7/4/17

Best Wishes

[signature]

INVASIVE SPECIES
PART THREE

INVASIVE SPECIES PART THREE

A little government job

Darlene and Logan Pollock

Library of Congress Control Number:		2016905101
ISBN:	Hardcover	978-1-5144-8043-4
	Softcover	978-1-5144-8042-7
	eBook	978-1-5144-8041-0

Print information available on the last page.

Rev. date: 04/30/2016

To order additional copies of this book, contact:
Xlibris
1-888-795-4274
www.Xlibris.com
Orders@Xlibris.com
739212

CHAPTER ONE

August, 2013

In a bedroom on the top floor of the Sovereign Hotel in Columbo, a man, a German, stretched and rolled over to the left until he was nearly lying on his belly. He was six feet tall and between fifty five and sixty years old. He liked the softness of the bed and the breeze coming through the patio door, on his nude body. In a few minutes he was sleeping again. In its' non-REM state, his brain didn't register the impact of the 158 grain slug as it smashed through his spine and his heart before fragmenting. His body's struggle with death ended in milliseconds. The killer approached and nudged him with the suppressor. Normally a professional didn't get that close to the 'Mark', but this time there were instructions to make sure of the job. Two hours later, the oblivious chambermaid came in to make the bed. She screamed and ran out into the hallway, screaming.

Nantucket Island- Late September 2013

Larry sat at a table in the Red Gull. A bald headed man, 5'10', who was approximately his age, came to his table and saluted him.

"We don't do those kinds of things anymore, Turnbull," Larry said, not looking at him. He was intentionally trying to ignore him and not practice any military courtesy.

"I always tried to show respect to a true hero," the former Admiral said.

"I remember this son-of-a-bitch making a real big deal about me carrying weapons in golf bag," Larry recalled the last time he had dealt with him. He was a Captain then.

"I over-reacted perhaps. May I sit here?"

"No, I don't feel like moving. Don't feel like talking either."

"I could have you put in security detention," Turnbull snapped.

"Don't go away mad...well, you know the rest," Larry countered.

The Admiral turned and walked away. Larry knew that whatever it was, this wasn't the end of the matter.

Early the next morning, Larry was sitting on their porch waiting for the sunrise. He saw a man on the sidewalk. He knew that it was General Tony Barber. Barber was a former Air Force guy. An intelligence officer that would get airsick on a merry-go-round. He turned and came up the walkway and came onto the porch.

"It is customary to stay off the porch until you are invited. What are you, a fucking Liberal?"

"Turnbull said you were being an asshole."

"He was the one always bucking for asshole. I suppose there's another way to get you off of our porch," Larry said as he stood up and motioned for Barber to follow him. He went down the steps and headed down the back driveway, toward the beach.

"It looks like a nice place. How's the wife?"

"There's too many influential and government types here. Nobody would appreciate getting the place shot-up all to hell."

"And the wife?"

"She doesn't like BlackOps and Spooks stinking up her porch either, Barbie."

"I've been in Nuclear Proliferation. We lost two packages, half megaton, Mark 28 type. It's in territorial waters of Sri Lanka, two thousand feet. Divers go down, but they haven't come up too good. We were hoping that you could help. It's possible that unfriendly people know where these bombs are at."

"You should find somebody that works for the government and you should find somebody that gives a shit."

"We could use some help here."

"Things are different now. I'm married, got a baby and a house," Larry said.

"Since when did that ever stop you? Do you know how many babies were on those airliners on 9/11?"

"I remember those news agency cameramen were filming Palestinians celebrating that 'great victory', so we know how they really feel about us now. If I see an Israeli tank run over a Palestinian woman or baby, I'm not gonna' feel bad about it. That's the way you gotta' fight a war, scalp for scalp," Larry said.

"It's a whole different ball game with Kerry and Clinton in charge down there," he said.

"It's the same game, the same players, the same horse shit. Nothing has changed. These fuckers can't pull their heads outta' their asses either."

"They're going back to the torturing prisoners thing, like that's doing any good."

"We were a lot smarter than that. We sure didn't take any pictures for the folks back home. Those guys really lacked for amusement," Larry said.

"We have to call the White House to flush a toilet," the general said.

"You chumps ain't got the Mossad to do your dirty work for you. Such a pity. Maybe they'll do it, for a price."

"We have looked at outside contractors. Nobody is interested," Barber said.

"I ain't either.

"I can't believe it. You really have changed!"

"It's called 'hope and change'. I really hope to hell that things change. There's no 'I' anymore, it's 'we' now. This time, God and country are not part of the deal," Larry stated as they got down to the beach.

———

"The fur seals are still hanging around. I guess they know the sharks aren't here," he added.

"I was looking at an Operations Report. It mentions a Palestinian woman and two children being methodically gunned down in the street."

"I remember hearing that when I was in Lebanon. All kinds of crazy things going on there," Larry said.

"The Muslims claimed it was a wedding."

"Somebody didn't get an invitation. In the Gaelic tradition, if any guest dies at the ceremony or the reception, the marriage is null and void and they have to do it all over again," Larry said.

"What a bummer."

"Never go to a Palestinian wedding," Larry joked.

"We want things to stay like they are."

"Like they are, where?"

"In Jerusalem."

"Jerusalem! Don't make me laugh. This Egyptian had this bar. He invited us to see a donkey show later that evening. The holiest city in the damn world, I couldn't believe it."

"The Muslims claim that Jerusalem is their sacred city. Mohammed rose into heaven from there."

"Just another fairy tale. God, those people believe anything. What was he doing in Jerusalem? Converting to Judaism? They don't even agree if their prophet is Mohammed or his nephew. I expect that some Muslim will be giving me some ridiculous explanation for Indianapolis being a sacred city for Islam," Larry said.

"Obama has changed the country forever they claim. Made it a paradise for illegals and people who won't work."

"Obama has just fucked it up more, a lot more, than any other president. Nobody changes the country, they just destroy the economy. Nixon changed it by taking us off the gold standard and Reagan changed it by starting these 401K's. Clinton got congress to rescind the Graham Leech Bliley laws and the Democrats claimed that Bush was a friend of banks when they know damn well that they did it," Larry said.

"You always liked to piss on somebody's parade. For reasons that I don't want to go into here, there are people, very highly placed people, that want to retrieve these packages without a lot of fanfare," he said.

"As you know, I'll tell anybody to pound salt."

"As we used to say-Failure is not an option."

"I have a new one for ya'-Not my problem," Larry said as he suddenly stopped.

"I'll be on the island for a couple days. I'm sure that I'll be seeing you again," Barber said.

"It's a small island. Too small for your kind of problems. I gotta' check on some laundry," Larry said then he walked landward without any word or gesture of parting.

These jerks just don't understand that this is 'free Amerikay', Larry thought. When he got to the laundry, the teenage girl at the counter looked at his ticket and told him that Linda wouldn't be in for a half an hour. He took a chair in the coin laundry in front and watched the sunrise over the ocean. A young man, who was about an inch taller than him, slim and with dark hair, sat down in the second chair to his left.

"It looks like another good sunrise," he said.

"Yes, very pretty," Larry said.

"My name is Clint."

"I'm Larry."

"My parents named me after the actor, not President Clinton."

"Yes, he was a tall, dark haired fellow like you."

"I'm picking up the linen for Regina's," Clint said.

"I'm just slummin'," Larry quipped.

"If you need a job, they're hiring busboys."

"Not at this time, but thank you anyways."

"What kind of work do you do?" he asked.

Larry decided to spare him the droll of the pilot plant.

"I'm a retired Navy diver."

Clint looked shocked.

"I...I'm sorry."

"Not at all. Your heart is in the right place, guy. That is a rare thing to see," Larry said.

"Are you the guy that lives on Seaside?"

"Yes, or rather, that's my wife's house."

"Wow, I've heard people talk about you and I've read about you in the paper, but I never thought I'd meet you," he said.

"How could you know? The newspaper used a picture of Misses Frobert. She looks nothing like me," Larry quipped.

They paused for a minute and watched a recap of mixed martial arts fighting on the TV.

"That was on pay per view. That Ronda takes out every opponent in the first round," Clint said.

Larry thought about the similarity in fighting philosophy. Forget convention, niceties and showmanship, just take out your opponent with the least time and effort possible. After a judo throw to get her opponent to the mat, she used an arm bar. The other woman realized that she would break her arm so she conceded immediately.

"What do you think of her?"

"She is one tough young lady. I don't think I'd want to engage in any physical activity where she was supposed to be beating the hell outta' me, if you know what I mean," Larry replied.

"I guess a lotta' guys are thinking about that."

Larry had become accustomed to women calling him a loser, but he hoped to never hear it from a woman that was beating the crap out of him. As he perused a diving magazine, he thought about what General Barber had said. There are approximately four hundred deep divers in the world. Only a few had been down to two thousand feet. Security clearances, heavy recovery know-how and somebody who wasn't currently on active service in the military, narrowed the field quite a bit, but Larry wouldn't even consider taking such a job. Nobody could talk him into that, he thought.

CHAPTER TWO

Larry decided to include a stroll through the cemetery on his evening walk. He saw a car at the side of the road, near the entrance. He instantly recognized the black man in an overcoat, looking down at the graves. He slowly turned his head and looked at him.

"Have you found some relatives?"

"This is a 'Whites Only' island," he remarked.

"Oh contrare! In the nineteenth century there were significant numbers of Blacks and Native Americans here," Larry informed him.

"I guess those were the 'good old days'."

"You better believe it."

"I understand that congratulations are in order. I also understand that there was a little Boo Boo," Tyrone said, still looking down at the graves.

"That's the way I've always worked. I've always had good luck in marriage, so I'm sticking with it."

"My daughter was born two years after we were married."

"See, I'm giving you a reason to feel superior. You can't beat that," Larry quipped.

"It's quite the contrary on this island."

"I had that problem. I publicly slammed a couple guys and now there's no more problems like that. Where's old 'Hairy Mission' at?"

"He took an overseas assignment," Tyrone said.

"He's probably sitting in some shithole cave in Afghanistan and you get to work here. What a lucky man you are."

"Why don't you just go and kill somebody. Mexican, Arab, Black, Asian, it doesn't matter to you!" McLeod snapped.

"I always thought we had Marines to do that. As you pointed out, those people are a geographical rarity here anyway."

"You can take the nigger outta' the jungle, but you can't have him on Nantucket?"

"Now you got it. You see, they'll start looking at real estate like the White House."

"Heaven forbid, Scarlett. I'm a house...I gotta' get comfortable using that word around whites."

"On 9/11, I was at a gas station. All these black people were in there blaming it on Bush. They were saying that gas would be three or four dollars a gallon by the next day. I told them that they were full of crap. They were telling me that it already was three or four dollars a gallon somewhere. I told them that that was bullshit. Just like the 'Obama money."

"It's three or four dollars now, so what's your point?" Tyrone asked.

"I'm glad you asked. After 9/11/2001, Barbara Boxer was saying that we need an Arab equivalent of the Cosby show. Evidently she feels that people are too stupid to know the difference between pop culture and reality. Nothing has changed. Seventy percent of the people in prison are still black, but the large majority must have huggable, cute children. So, I got this idea to make these execution drugs and tell people that it turns the malefactor into a zombie. Everybody will think it's cool then."

"What if they don't think it's cool?"

"Just like Napoleon, set up the cannons on the Capital steps and when the malcontents start rioting-Boom, canister shot at close range. The liberals become much better behaved when they're subjected to canister shot at close range."

"It sounds like Hitler to me." Tyrone said.

"No, it's nothing like Hitler. Hitler was a disgruntled nutball from the First World War. He just took the old ideas of Jew hating and applied them to a much broader range of people. People that he blamed for their defeat in the First World War. He relied on some fellow wackos like Himmler. This idea of the Aryan race was hogwash. A Wagnerian tale that the blonde haired blue eyed Germans had defeated the Romans in the Teutoburgerwald. It was nothing but a beauty contest. There is absolutely no reason to believe that these 'Aryans' are in any way physically or intellectually superior to other people. They fudged the test results and beat to death anybody who tried to dispute them," Larry explained.

"So if it wasn't jews and socialist, who was responsible for Germany's defeat?"

"Why it was those datburn Smedley Butler Marines. At least they always got the credit for it. Pershing elected to do the old 'Indian Fighting' method. Bombard them suckers at night then sneak up on them right before dawn. The guys are exposed to enemy fire for a much shorter time that way. You just have to watch out for things like mustard gas. They should have cut the balls off those kraut bastards for using gas."

"So, what's wrong with socialism?"

"If you have a piddling little country like Sweden or Norway, you might try to pull it off. Unfortunately, piddling little countries get run over real quick by people like Hitler and Stalin. You see, the fundamental flaw in the socialist system is that it exists like a covered fish tank. Nobody else can come in. European countries have much more restrictive immigration laws. In fact they don't like to let anybody in. Here, we had a free enterprise system that welcomed everybody. You see, we can't have it both ways. There would be a billion people here by next year," Larry explained.

"So is there anything good about it that we can use?"

"Sure, everybody has to keep an automatic rifle or submachine gun in their house."

"I hate to ask this, but what can I take away from this?" Tyrone asked.

"Very simple, when it comes time to put your foot down, you put your foot down on somebody's neck. You don't need to explain why because you're working for the 'Man' and the man is Uncle Sam. In that respect, it sucks being a civilian."

"Great talking with you, Chief."

"Don't take any Lamprey Eels," Larry said then he continued on his way.

That Tyrone is a real corker. The CIA is no outfit to be worried about race. Any person should be thought of as being in your outfit or in some other outfit. Larry wanted to be his friend, but Turnbull and Barber could go stuff themselves and get the hell off this island, Larry thought.

Larry was sitting on the couch when Shirley came in with Althea in the stroller.

"There you are, Sweetie. Have you got mommy all straightened out now?" Larry asked the baby as he picked her up out of the stroller.

"She's a little charmer, just like her daddy. I can't tell her no."

"That's easy, we just bite those mommy cheeks," Larry said as he kissed her baby cheeks.

Althea laughed at that.

"I ran into Ed Tate. Carrie is four months along," Shirley said as she bent down.

"MMMmmmMMM," Larry said as he kissed Shirley.

"We know what they been doin'. Yeah we do. You'll have a little neighbor to play with," Larry told the baby.

"She went to Doctor Liebermann. According to him, her Fallopian tubes were so damaged by the Chlamydia she had as a teenager that she couldn't conceive."

"Another doctor that won't talk to us. It works every time," Larry said while setting the baby in her playpen.

"The medical opinion is that the tubes regenerated sufficiently."

"No thanks to ten years of treatment and forty thousand dollars wasted," Larry said.

"Doctors in the prestigious New England Journal of Medicine give all the credit to the Shawl belonging to Larry Mayer. Note the obvious medical qualities of the garment," Shirley quipped.

"A bastion of Yankee ignorance! Ed and Carrie are happy with the result, so everybody else oughta' be."

"You know doctors. They'll want to take it apart fiber by fiber."

"Tell Melanie to bitch slap any doctor that tries to touch it. It can't be tampered with in any way."

"Excluding me, that's five women so far. It's getting to be quite a local legend and a real draw for their shop.

"Make sure they keep it in the safe at night," Larry said.

"What about those jokers you were talking about?"

"Two Hydrogen bomb from an aircraft carrier, in two thousand feet of water."

"Somebody took them out to dust them? Those are kept in the security magazines five decks down. They don't just fall off the deck," Shirley stated.

"They have had accidents during training exercises. It's deep enough that recovery is problematic. I ain't doing it. I told them to go away and stay away."

"I'm glad you told them to take a hike. Two thousand feet is just too much. No saturation dives for you, Chief," Shirley said as he sat down.

"They could use an atmospheric diving suit. There is one called the ADS 2000 Newtsuit. It is suitable for that depth."

"Is it safe?"

"You can't say 'safe' at that depth. Just like flying, it's a risk activity."

"What's the fatality rate per incident?"

"Even with that equipment, it's not good," Larry replied.

On a boat, General Barber got a phone call------

"Yes...Yes, a one and a half second delay. I'm ready...Yes, Al...Roger that, everybody is here now... No, no problem with the South Africans... Everybody will cooperate when they see the money... Apache, we're using him as the number two. We'll give him a new name...Operation Jerusalem is on track. We have the money already. Absolutely, in Morocco...No problem... I know Mayer, he is not one to be afraid. One or two days should do it...I'll let you know when...I'll take care of it when we arrive... Roger, out."

The next morning, Larry was sitting on the porch with Althea. Saul Muenster, the accountant, came up the walk.

"Saul, you old son of a sea cook, how the hell ya' doing?"

"Fine, is Shirley in?"

"Never mind about that, come over here and play with the baby. Boo Boo, this is Uncle Saul. Yes, he was born in that suit and with that sour puss. Give old Uncle Saul a bite on the cheek....Oh no, daddy! I'll get some nasty yuppie disease. I'll start believing all the crap they tell me at Harvard!" Larry said in a puppet voice.

"I really must see Shirley," Saul said.

"You really gotta' loosen up, guy. Ally will show ya'," Larry said as he lifted her to her feet and she tried to walk.

"Dan-cin' yeah, dan-cin' yeah," Larry sang as he gently turned her from side to side.

"Yes, that's very amusing...."

"Saul, you can come in," Shirley said from the open door.

"Don't keep him too long, Baby. The boss and I gotta' teach him to boogie," Larry said as Saul went into the house.

An hour later the baby had fallen asleep, so Larry carried her to the dining room annex where there was a bed for her. They passed Shirley's study and the door was open. Saul was in there by himself.

"Uncle Saul wore you out," Larry said as he walked by the doorway.

After he put her to bed, he heard a neighbor playing the opening movement to the New World Symphony. Going back the way he came, he saw that Saul was still busy on his calculator. This is too good to pass up, he thought.

"Saul, that's the New World Symphony!"

"So it is."

"That was Dvorak."

"I never studied music, I'm afraid," he replied.

"Dvorak was a Bohemian!"

"And this means?"

"Bohemians don't write symphonies!"

"I see."

"Bohemians write polkas. They can't write symphonies!!"

"It's called 'thinking outside the box', Chief," Shirley said from behind him.

"Oh yes, I suppose that's the Bohemian way. Steal the idea from somebody else. Ally is sleeping."

"We'll be another hour. I told Rosa to forget supper. We'll meet Frank and Jane at Fog Island."

"Good, maybe they're serving Crow tonight. Why don't you join us, Saul?" Larry quipped.

"Call your friend and stay out of trouble," Shirley said then she walked into her study.

"You must have me confused with that guy in the navy."

Larry arrived at Fog Island early to meet his old college buddy, Louis Gibb. Unexpectedly General Barber, another man about forty and a woman about 28 years old came to his table. Since there was a woman, he stood.

"Larry, this is Lauren Ball and Hugh Kirby. This is Larry Mayer," Barber introduced them.

"Sorry you have to run. Nice meeting you."

"May we join you?"

"Afraid not, I have some real friends coming," Larry snapped.

"Some other time then," Barber said and they left.

Gibb arrived after Shirley and the others got there. They all stood.

"Frank and Jane Folger, this is Lou Gibb, a former classmate and cousin-in-law of mine," Larry introduced them.

"Nice meeting you, Lou," Frank said as they shook hands.

"Same here," Lou said.

"Sit down here and tell us what you've been up to," Larry said.

"Absolutely nothing! I'm a welfare recipient. I sent the wife back to work and I wile away the hours trying to write something that I can sell," Lou said as they all sat down.

"Well, money can't buy you happiness."

"I've always heard that...from people with no money."

"Lou is just about the craziest guy that I have ever seen. He is the only guy I ever knew who has been to the Playboy mansion," Larry said.

They looked at Lou.

"I was a pilot for Hugh Heffner. I gave it up after two years. Every time I was at one of those parties, I lost a year of my life."

"So, you could forget about Kent State. No big loss," Larry quipped.

"Unfortunately, I had no control over what part got erased."

"Apparently you were the only one there who ever worried about that. I remember when you flew those playmates to Las Vegas," Larry said.

"Yeah, ten women and their luggage from Lake Geneva in a 402. You can't short the fuel and fly overloaded, anymore. Big airports don't allow anything that they don't have to allow, for sure."

"We were in Flight school together. What a riot that was. His instructor died on him while doing the touch and goes," Larry said.

"I thought he was sleeping, so I landed. Later on the ambulance gets there and they're saying that he's gone, which was obvious enough already. This EMP is asking me all kinds of questions. I tell him that I was trying to fly the plane, so I didn't really notice when the guy croaked. You can't believe how hard it was for people to believe that. Of course, then the FAA had to jump in on it because it happened while the plane was flying. I told them that I thought he was sleeping and I was coming in to land anyway, so the time was the same."

"That's very interesting," Jane opined.

"Men will talk about anything," Shirley said.

"He's got a million of them," Larry said.

"It seems that without an instructor, you were in big trouble," Frank said.

"Well, they couldn't take away my PPL, because technically I didn't have one. I suppose they could have tried to fine me for flying without an instructor, but technically there was an instructor there in body if not in spirit," Lou quipped.

"I was on a 737 and we were coming into Denver and an engine quit then the landing gear was giving us trouble. The airport was on emergency red alert and the pilot can't land because the wheels aren't locking down, so the pilot tells us that they will keep raising and lowering the landing gear in an attempt to get landing gear locked down properly. So, for a half an hour we're flying at a thousand feet above the ground on one engine, circling while the cockpit crew is raising and lowering the landing gear," Frank said.

"I take it that you made it down okay," Lou said.

"Oh yes. On the fourth attempt, the landing gear locked down okay and we landed into the wind with no problem at all. Later on, I heard the pilot or co-pilot say that being low on fuel actually helped us stay in the air, since the weight was reduced."

"I'm sure you wouldn't want to get too low on fuel," Larry quipped.

"That must have been about the time they legalized marijuana," Jane said.

"Welcome to the friendly skies. Your flight deck crew were flying at 40,000 feet before they ever get in the airplane," Frank joked.

"What John Denver called the 'Rocky Mountain High'."

"I'll avoid Denver," Shirley said.

"So, you two met a Kent state?" Jane asked.

"Yes, I was shocked to find out that he and Darla were cousins. I wouldn't have believed that they came from the same planet," Larry joked.

"There was never a dull moment with Larry in the class. He never let anybody get away with anything. It didn't endear him to the professors any, but poor Darla always loved him."

"Speaking of which, how's the family doing?" Larry asked.

***

"They started borrowing money then they started having problems paying it back, but that doesn't seem to deter them from borrowing more whenever they feel like it."

"You don't lend money to children. They never pay it back. Daddy still owes them a living," Larry said.

"Where was this guy $145,000 ago," Louis said.

"So, you're meeting an agent up here?"

"Yeah, she won't get back from New York until tomorrow morning, she says."

"Is this a hard sell?" Larry asked.

"No, I got everything here, manuscript, illustrations, the works. They never believe me. Everybody else bothers their agent when they have an idea for a book, so the agent can't believe that all she has to do is hand it off to the production editor. How much easier can I make it?"

"So you are trying to sell a book?" Frank asked.

"I can't sell ice water in hell. The publisher has to market and publicize the book. I go around to book signings and talk to people. Those 'lunch with the author' tours suck. I never get a damn thing to eat," Lou complained.

"Promise them that this book will sell," Larry quipped.

"I should write college texts. Guaranteed sales and grossly exorbitant prices," Lou countered.

"It's like the three laws of Thermodynamics. You can't win, you can't break even, you can't quit playing the game," Larry said.

"You know that you can't believe anything those professors tell you. I'm surprised that an old Midwest conservative like you can live up here," Lou said.

At dinner, Larry was handed a message by the waiter. It was a request to meet Miss Ball and Mister Kirby on the patio. Larry put it in his pocket and ignored it.

The next morning he got a phone call from a woman with a British accent. As soon as she mentioned Hugh Kirby, he hung up. An hour later, he got a call from a man who refused to identify himself. He claimed that he had one hour to cooperate or they would get a court order to have him brought to the police station for questioning. Larry told him to have Hugh Kirby meet him at the cemetery in an hour. His next call was to Tyrone McLeod.

Although it was not warm, Larry took the scooter. He parked it inside the fence and waited. A dark gray BMW arrived a few minutes later. Lauren and Hugh got out and walked toward him.

"Nice seeing you again, Mister Mayer," Hugh said, holding out his hand.

"Not really," Larry said, disdaining to shake hands.

"I don't think you understand. We are the good guys here."

"I don't care what you say you are. I couldn't give a shit less," Larry snapped.

"We don't have the time to get you up to speed. You'll have to trust us."

Larry thought about Joe Cole ending up on the bottom of the ocean by trusting the wrong people.

"I don't know most of you and I sure in the hell don't trust any of those I do know. Mountain climbers say that you can rope yourself to a guy or you can't. It's the same way in diving."

"I was a mountain climber in my school days," Hugh said.

An idiot climbs mountains, Larry thought.

"I wouldn't do things like climb mountains because there's nothing tangible to bring back."

Larry saw Tyrone coming up the path.

"Hey, Ty," Larry said.

"There's my nigga'," Tyrone greeted him.

"There's my Marine."

Larry hoped that he could count on him.

"So, where was I? Oh yeah, I don't dig foreigners trying to buffalo me in my own country. Fuck off!"

"I am a representative of Her Majesty's government. I act in the interest of the British government and the British people."

"Look down, Kirby. See that? That's not your country and I'm not some fucking Irish peasant that you can whip or machinegun. You haven't told me who you work for and I don't give a shit. The answer is no. I'm not interested. I don't care. I don't know you and I don't care what you're selling and I sure in the hell don't care for any fucking British government. Is there anything that I said that you don't understand?"

"Mike Hart had quite a different impression of you."

"That was another fucked up operation that involved killing a bunch of Africans that we should have avoided and stealing a military aircraft that belonged to an unfriendly country. Not something to brag about in the UN."

"All well that ends well, I suppose."

"They teach you stupid things in British Public Schools. First thing you always ask yourself-what law, if any, has been broken here? Last thing you ask yourself-what, if anything, have we learned here?"

"I can't understand why anybody would have you on an operation?"

"Because I'm not some pug British prick asshole."

"I have had just about enough from you, Mister Mayer!!" Hugh snapped as he looked like he was about to throw a punch. Larry punched him in the stomach and in the neck, below the ear. A rapid combination of blows that always takes them by surprise. As he hit the ground, Larry was ready with a follow-up kick.

"Freeze, Mayer!" Lauren yelled as she pulled a SIG.

When Larry turned toward her, he was surprised to see Tyrone strike downward on her right arm, knocking the gun away and putting her in a choke hold from behind.

"Let the white boys have their fun. I'll keep you entertained," Tyrone said.

Larry picked up her automatic.

"Pick up your boyfriend, and you two get the hell off this island," Larry said.

Everyone was quiet as Lauren helped Hugh to his feet and they limped back to their car.

"Thanks for the assist, guy," Larry said as he handed the gun to McLeod.

"Typical Black guy, always goes for the white woman," Tyrone said.

"Conventional, but effective if the opponent is smaller and weaker."

"Is that what you really think?"

"Maybe she'll enjoy it more the next time," Larry quipped.

"You're a real sick bastard. Does anybody like you?"

"Althea likes me. I bite her baby cheeks and she laughs."

"This isn't our outfit, I can tell you that," Tyrone stated when they got to his car.

"Well, if you can't tell me then tell 'Brown Noser' to call me. I need some information here."

"I'll see what I can do, Chief," he said as he got into his car.

As Larry got on the scooter, he saw old Misses Bradford looking at him strangely.

"Hello Misses Bradford. We gotta' keep sending those bastards back to England like our ancestors did," Larry said, smiling.

"Yes, I suppose so," she said while looking unhappy.

Later that day, when Larry returned, Shirley was on the phone. She wrote a note to go ahead with supper. When Larry was done with supper, she was still on the phone. Larry gave the baby a bottle then rocked her until she fell asleep. Shirley came in looking unhappy.

"I thought the phone was gonna' meltdown," Larry said.

"An old navy buddy, Flight Officer Amelia Bell, has an older brother, Paul Bell. His former wife and two daughters, Christine and Connie, are living in Virginia. Connie got involved with a guy who got her using cocaine. He was physically abusing her and blackmailing her. The police weren't doing anything about it, so Christine emptied a .38 special into him. She got twenty five years in prison in Virginia."

"Yeah, prosecutors get enthusiastic about that sometimes. I guess she'll have to try an appeal."

"Her appeal was denied. They kept her out of prison until the conviction. They have talked to the governor, congressmen, everything. Can't you help her?"

"I sure in the hell don't have any friends like that," Larry stated.

"That General Barber and Admiral Turnbull are lackeys in the State Department. Bootlicks for the Secretary of State and her flunkies. Maybe you can cut a deal with them," she suggested.

"I've been giving them the 'Three Stooges' act. I don't think that we can go back to playing nice now. I know that this is on the other side of the world, but I haven't any idea what else is going down. It will mean some time away from home," Larry said.

"This is Christine's only chance. I wouldn't ask if it didn't mean that her whole life was shot to hell."

"For one thing, they'll have to come looking for me. I can't be dealing from a position of weakness and I don't think that I'll be hearing from them again. Even those jerks get a message when it's delivered with some violence. Give me her name and prison number and I'll see what I can do."

Shirley wrote-Christine Yvette Bell, VDC-101-1045, and handed it to Larry.

An hour later, Larry was walking downtown when he ran into an unhappy General Barber.

"Hello, general, fall is definitely on the way," Larry remarked.

Barber gave him a nasty look.

"Mister Public School was gonna' hit me like I was some Irish peasant. Big mistake as you know."

Barber had no response.

"In 1781, they savaged the coast around here. I was just getting some back for the Revolutinary war. You can put that on your report. Er-uh, I take it that you write some kinda' reports here," Larry said.

"Something like that."

"Nice car. I would have preferred Mackinac Island. There are no cars there, only horses."

"Would you like a ride home?" Barber asked.

"To the south side of the island if you would."

"Turn right," Larry said when they got to the end of that road.

Barber turned right and they headed down the dirt road which went nowhere. He knew that the road would end on a large sand beach.

"There's nothing down here," he said when he stopped the car where the sand began.

"That's because men leave nothing alone. It's always out there, where people can't go, I find things. I suppose that you know about the Piper Arrow that had Joe Cole and Luis Valero and the three guys that I recovered from the wreck of the Sweet Pea?"

"Yes, I have seen the FAA and Coast Guard reports."

"I can't believe you guys. Let me tell you a little story-When General Ushijima took over command on Okinawa, the brig was full. He went to the brig himself and let the men out and ordered them into formation. He told them that he didn't want any discipline problems in his outfit and he told them to go back to their units. The stars on his arm didn't mean anything. He still understood his men like a brass bar Lieutenant."

"Maybe we got off on the wrong foot."

"You've wrong-footed every move here, but you're persistent, I'll give you that," Larry said.

"So, what do you want, money?"

"Do you think that I ever dived below sixty feet for money? I want a pardon for Christine Y. Bell. She's in prison in Virginia."

"Is she a relative?"

"No, I have never met her in fact," Larry informed him.

"I'll have to check into this. I can't promise anything."

"She ventilated this lowlife that was destroying her sister with drugs, blackmail and physical abuse. Don't give her a medal, just get her out for good then we can move on this," Larry said.

"It will definitely happen after this operation," Barber said.

"Before this operation. I don't leave home until she leaves prison for good," Larry stated.

He knew about people's penchant for forgetting about favors owed and it was real easy for people who are that high up.

"I'll have to make some calls. This could take a day or two."

"I got as much time as you do," Larry said.

Two days later, Shirley got a phone call informing her that the conviction of Christine Bell had been vacated by the prosecutor. Her mother and father and sister would be there when she walked out of prison later that day. They had been instructed to say nothing to anybody about the affair. They didn't even know the name of Shirley or Larry Mayer. Larry was on an airplane to Norfolk, Virginia by that time. Barber sent a message-'The new cook is on the way."

CHAPTER THREE

When he got to Norfolk, the diving vessel, USS Carlson was there. It was similar to the Marine Challenger deep diving vessel that they would board in Sri Lanka. For several days, most of the crew were taken off and Larry and Commander Holscomb's 'crew' did a shakedown with the ADS 2000 Newtsuit in the diving well. It was somewhat heavier and more sophisticated than the hardsuits that he had used in trials in his navy days. In those days, they had taken the lighter ADS 1000 suit to two thousand feet without difficulty. They practiced controlling the Remote Recovery Vehicle and lifting various objects from the bottom. The 'crew' was shown line drawings of the Mark 28 nuclear weapon. They were cylindrical, eight and a half feet long and twenty two inches in diameter. The RRV on the marine challenger would have a grab with jaws specifically designed to lift the bombs. Since it was designed to operate at a depth of two miles, there should be no problems with it at two thousand feet.

On the fifth day, they packed their bags and took an airliner to an airport in Morocco then on to India. A C-130 took them to Sri Lanka and there were military trucks to take them to Trincomalee, on the east coast. The Marine Challenger was supposed to be a vessel for oil rig work, so it had a full time crew. Most of the crew couldn't come, so they were sequestered ashore for the duration. For the next two days, more preparations were done. The forward half of two twenty one inch Dummy Torpedos, filled with sand, would be the simulated bombs. An area that was a thousand feet deep and had a flat, sandy bottom, was chosen for the tests. Larry, and everybody else, seemed to be happy with the operation so far. That evening he was at mess with the diving crew. His Top Man (Dive Controller) was also a former diving chief named Scott Donnelly. He sat across from him.

"So, we leave tomorrow at sunset," Scott said.

"Bright eyed and clear headed," Larry said.

"You retired in '96?"

"Yes, I was washed out for medical reasons."

"That was a year after I joined. I was in for ten years then I left to get married."

"To work in some damn factory in Ohio," Larry quipped.

"On oil rigs. Choose your outfit, choose your dives, take care of your family. That's the life...except it wasn't much of a life for us, I'll tell ya'."

"But you took care of your family?"

"When I had a family, I suppose. When they were gone, there wasn't much use to that," Scott said.

"If I hadn't been doing fleet duty, I'm sure I'd have run into you."

"You didn't get into pro diving?"

"No, our families lived in northeast Ohio, so Darla wanted to move back there. Diving just became a hobby."

"You have been pulling off some real good dives in the last couple of years, I hear."

"A couple in the Thousand Islands and a couple on Nantucket. Nothing for any money, I'm afraid," Larry replied.

"We're getting flat fees here, no percentages."

"I'm getting nothing but expenses paid. It's a favor to help out a friend of a relative."

"That's a real stretch for two thousand feet of water."

"They see it as twenty five years in prison for a one day dive. They think they're the ones being generous here," Larry explained.

"They can think what they like when they're a half mile down in the murky. I don't like working at night and I don't like those LED's. There's too many things, like squids, that are active at night in these waters," Scott said.

"The LED's are a pain, but they can't be seen quite so easily by ships, airplanes and satellites that might be in the vicinity. Anyone who sees the lights will think that we're a much smaller fishing vessel."

That night, Barber sent a message-'The new cook has arrived."

The next night, the Marine Challenger left the dock at 21:15 hours. In less than an hour, they were at the location where the dummy 'bombs' had been dropped. They lowered the Remote Recovery Vehicle and searched the bottom for two hours before they located their 'objects'. They pulled up the RRV and repositioned their ship so that it was nearly directly over the 'objects'. The 'crew' suited up Larry for a trial dive at that depth. They did everything according to the check lists and it took forty minutes before he was ready to lower. He was lifted and lowered by a cable/umbilical with fiber optic cords for communication and monitoring conditions in the hardsuit. When he was near the bottom, he turned on the lights. He could see that he about ten feet off the bottom.

"Five feet per minute," Larry requested.

"Five FPM, roger that," Scott relayed.

He set the feet gently on the bottom. The buoyancy was still nearly neutral at this point.

"On the bottom," Larry reported.

"Roger that. Primary and redundant life support functions are green. Zero point two one bars oxygen and constant. Twenty two degrees internal and humidity decreasing. What's your status?"

"Looking good. The bottom is solid and flat. I see the 'objects' now. They appear to be undamaged. It should be no problem using the grab on them." He practiced with various hand tools for an hour then he came up.

Once on deck, he was unsuited and checked by the doctor. Everyone seemed happy and ready for tomorrow when the diver and the RRV would be working in concert to grab onto the 'objects' and bring them to the surface. He slept for the remainder of that night and woke up at 1300 hours. Scott and Harold Havers, the tech specialist, were at mess when he got to the galley.

"Hi guys. Where's your partners in crime?" Larry asked as he sat down.

"Albert and Dale have already eaten. They're probably sleeping somewhere," Scott replied.

"Were you in Lebanon?" Hal asked.

"Yes, I was."

"I overheard Holscomb saying that you killed a lot of people there. Hundreds in fact."

"I don't know the exact number," Larry said.

"Reprisals for all those dead heroes?" Hal asked.

"Regrettably, they were not heroes, they were targets. I used the PLO backed Muslim extremists for my targets. I knew to fight like they did and took scalp for scalp. President Reagan decorated me for that. He also decorated me for operations in Grenada. Reagan was a great guy."

"You were one of the guys that pioneered the deep saturation dives in the mid-seventies?"

"Yes, I was doing that, but there were others doing it too," Larry replied.

"What made you do that?" Scott asked.

"Free divers were going below five hundred feet on a breath of air, so we figured that something had to be done here. Different mixtures were tried in pressure chambers and we had theoretical mixtures that would work below a thousand feet. The problem was to find someone foolish enough to do it."

"So you were the lab rats?" Hal asked.

"There were four guys that tried it before me and Hartmann. Those four didn't make out too good, though."

"Explain 'not too good'," Scott requested.

"Three died and one was crippled badly by an embolism. He killed himself later. Hartmann and I ended up completing the trials and setting depth records. It was a great operation and I really enjoyed working with him."

Later, Larry worked out on the treadmill and did light stretching and weight work with the other guys. After supper there was a briefing and a discussion attended by General Barber and Commander Holscomb. Several technical questions were brought up and the solutions were found before they quit the meeting. Afterward, Larry hung around on deck with his topside crew.

"I remember hearing a story about the curse of ten sixty three. Have you ever heard of that?" Havers asked.

"Mark 5 helmet number 76-1063 on the tender Hancock. I heard that the three men who dived with it before me had died in it. I used it for a year and a half. I used no other helmet but 1063, for my fifty two dives, with no problem at all. The first guy that dived with it after me, died in it. The captain had the whole thing, Helmet, Corselet, Jake suit, weights, everything, thrown overboard."

"You said that you live on Nantucket Island?" Albert asked.

"Yes, I do now."

"Where did you live before?" he asked.

"Boston Mills, Ohio."

"Why did you move to Nantucket? That doesn't seem like your kinda' place."

"My wife always lived there and she likes it there."

"I wouldn't live on an island. I could have lived on an island in Maine for cheap, but it's a different story in the winter time. You live on dried fish, corn bread and beans for five months, just like the pioneers. No phone before the advent of cellphones. Electricity was supplied by an underwater cable. No gas or sewer. Heaven help you if you got sick, there's no hospital there," Albert said.

"This guy has the 'wrong stuff'," Hal joked.

"This is a long way from Casco Bay. We won't worry about frozen fingers here," Larry said.

"All those people on Nantucket go to Florida in the wintertime," Hal said.

"I'm the one that doesn't," Larry quipped.

"How do you afford it? Do you live on Easy street?" Scott asked jokingly.

"On Seaside road. Shirley's grandfather bought the property originally then left it to her father and her father passed it on to her," Larry explained.

"Her father died?" Hal asked.

"No, her mother died. Wife number two wanted Long Island, so Shirley got the house early," Larry explained.

"Have you done any diving at home?" Albert asked.

"Just nailing sharks and bringing up dead people."

"There should be a lot of shipwrecks around there," he said.

"The whole damn thing is sand. Anything that is on the bottom eventually gets covered by sand," Larry explained.

Shortly after sunset they got the word to suit up. Larry lowered himself into the lower half of the suit and they assembled the sections around him. When all the checks had been done on the life support system, the face plate was secured and they went through the check list again. When everything checked out okay, Larry and diving suit were lifted, swung overboard and lowered into the water. When he was on the bottom, they went through the checklist again and Larry was satisfied.

"Okay, send down the Rove."

"Roger that. Rove in position and lowering," Scott replied.

It took twenty minutes to lower the RRV. Larry could see its lights because they were pointed almost straight down. When it was ten feet from the bottom, Larry saw a problem.

"Stop lowering," he ordered.

"Roger that, lowering stopped," Scott said.

Larry looked at the underside again.

"Open the grab."

"The grab is open," Scott replied.

"Negative, it is not open."

"Repositioning Camex," Scott said as he saw the camera move.

"I'll try opening and closing the jaws," Scott said after a minute.

Larry saw no movement of the jaws or the hydraulic lines.

"Can you see anything, Chief?"

"Nothing is moving here," Larry replied.

"There must be a failure in the hydraulic system. We'll have to bring the Rove up."

"Roger that. When you get the Rove up then bring me up."

"Roger that, Chief," Scott said.

It took a half hour to get the RRV up on deck then they pulled Larry up. The crew unsuited him and they went to the mess for an early breakfast. They stayed out that day since they weren't anywhere near the real bombs and the Rove technicians were sure that they could fix the problem. Larry went to his quarters and got some sleep. He woke up at eleven o'clock local time. He had been dreaming that he was in a hotel room on Hawaii. The ship was hardly moving at all and somewhere nearby the Hawaiian sunset song was being played. Larry washed up then went out on deck. The crew was working on the Rove.

"What did you do to my machine?" Hal quipped.

"Trying to get the son of a bitch to work."

"Here's the problem, the hydraulic return valve. It was stuck closed so that fluid couldn't flow through the lines. There's sixteen valves here and the only one that would shut it down, failed," he said as he handed it, wrapped in a rag, to Larry.

"Yeah, that's always the way it is," Larry said as he looked at it.

"We're bleeding the lines now. We'll double check everything here and we'll get you later for the suit check. I want to check the batteries and recharge the absorber/regenerator. We might as well check everything while we're at it," Hal said.

"Yeah, good deal," Larry agreed.

After lunch, they brought out the suit and checked everything as agreed. The batteries, pressure tanks and air regenerator unit were attached to the back of the suit and would be subjected to 60 atmospheres or 882 psi of pressure. The fittings and tubing were rated at 10,000 psi pressure. Everything was working well, so Larry didn't allow the equipment to be disassembled. An atmospheric purge was done on the air regenerator unit until the suit was needed later.

After sunset, Larry got into the lower half of the suit and the rest of it was assembled around him. After attaching the faceplate, going over the checklist took another twenty minutes then Larry was lowered into the water. When he got to the bottom, he turned on the lights and located the 'dummies'. He told them that he was ready and they began lowering the RRV. Even at a thousand feet, he could see the lights as soon as the Rove entered the water. He felt something bump him from the back then he saw a squid swim by on his right. It turned around and came at him again. He was unable to turn his body, but he extended his arm with the clamp open and the squid struck the clamp and then beat a hasty retreat.

"Try chewing on this, sucker!"

"We didn't copy that," Scott said.

"Just a hungry squid."

"Let's us know if there's a problem."

"Will do," Larry replied.

When the RRV was only a couple feet off the bottom, Larry turned it to line up the grab for the pick up.

"Lower at one FPM," he requested.

"Lowering at one FPM," Scott acknowledged.

In a couple minutes, the Rove was right on the dummy.

"Stop lowering," Larry ordered.

"Stop lowering."

"Engage the grab."

"Engaging the grab," Scott acknowledged.

Larry saw the jaws of the grab close on the dummy and lift it an inch or two.

"The grab is working good now. Lift the RRV four feet."

"Lifting the RRV," Scott said.

It raised up slowly then stopped where Larry wanted it. He secured the safety bar then moved away.

"Safety is on. Raise the RRV to the surface."

"Roger that, raising the Rove."

Larry watched the recovery vehicle as it was raised to the surface. It was carrying a ton and a half more weight, but it could handle that easily. In twenty minutes it broke the surface and Larry couldn't see the lights anymore. He waited ten minutes.

"Scott, is everything alright?"

"Scott is away for now. They're having some problem with a cable on the RRV," a voice said.

"Call me every five minutes and keep me informed."

"Will do."

It took an hour before the cable problem was fixed. Larry waited patiently while they worked on it topside.

"Sorry Chief. We had a kink in a cable, so we reeled it off and replaced the whole length of it," Scott explained when he got back to the phone.

"Okay, if you're ready, send it down again."

"Roger that, Chief. We'll have it in the water in five minutes."

"Very good," Larry acknowledged.

Once the RRV was in the water, everything went smoothly and Larry helped maneuver it into position and made sure that the grab held the dummy properly before it was raised to the surface. When the RRV was secure on deck, Larry was brought up. Nearly everyone was there when they took off the faceplate.

"How are you feeling, Chief?" Scott asked.

"I feel like I'm carry a lotta' extra weight," Larry quipped.

"We'll have you outta' there in a jiffy."

It still took twenty minutes to dismantle the suit and get Larry pulled out of it. He went to the head even before the doctor examined him. Back out on deck, Commander Holscomb watched while the doctor examined him.

Larry hadn't talked to him much since the commander seemed to prefer to go through Scott, as the Dive Controller.

"Everything went fairly well, Chief," Holscomb said.

"Yes, we got what we came for."

"There's a debriefing in thirty minutes."

"Roger that," Larry said.

Since the 'payoff' dive was scheduled for tomorrow night, the ship headed back to Trincomalee. Once ashore, there was only one local watering hole that they could visit and they had to leave by eleven o'clock. Larry and Scott were invited to a welcoming reception for somebody in the State Department that evening. An airplane took them to Columbo and a car took them to a hotel where they changed into evening wear. Larry's best suit wasn't nearly up to the occasion, but he went anyway. The host, a Ralph Putzer, wanted to meet him.

When he arrived, he tried to find Putzer, to introduce himself as is customary, but he was told that Putzer was unavailable. He got a drink and found Scott talking to some young women in long evening gowns.

"Larry Mayer, this is Virginia, Dakota and Montana."

"Three outta' fifty ain't bad," Larry quipped.

"Larry is the most gutsy diver in this world, barring none."

"He has a penchant for understatement," Larry said, smiling.

"It must be very exciting work," Virginia suggested.

"Tomorrow night, Larry will be at two thousand feet. That's deeper than anybody else has gone and lived to tell about it."

"Is it scary at that depth?" Montana asked.

"I wouldn't go down if it was."

"Don't let him bamboozle you, ladies. That's sixty atmospheres, 882 pounds per square inch. He's only an inch away from being crushed to death at any moment."

"Why do you do it?" Virginia asked.

"So I don't have to wear a suit and tie," Larry quipped.

"I have to wear a stock tie when riding. I don't like them either," Virginia said.

"I wonder who invented the tie?" Dakota asked.

"It was first used in the Thirty Years War. They used hastily conscripted peasants as infantry. Since one peasant looks like another, they gave them ties to distinguish them," Larry explained.

"If you don't mind me saying, you look a little old for diving," Montana said.

"Unfortunately, Tom Cruise and Clark Gable were unavailable."

She looked at him quizzically.

"Most people think that Navy divers have to look like Tom Cruise or Clark Gable," Larry explained.

"Are you in the navy?" Montana asked.

"No, I was forced to retire in '96."

"He wouldn't wear a tie in the navy either," Scott quipped.

"Do you get paid a lot for doing this?" Virginia asked.

"I get paid nothing. This is a favor for somebody. Somebody that I don't even know," Larry replied.

"Can you elaborate?"

"A relative was a shipmate of a woman back in '94. The woman has a brother who was married, but not anymore. His former wife and two daughters are living in Virginia. Some lowlife guy got one daughter using cocaine and abused her and blackmailed her. The other daughter took a gun and settled his hash for good. She got twenty five years, so I made a deal, she walks and I dive," Larry explained.

The three women looked at him for a moment.

"Wow, that is real chivalry!" Montana said.

"You don't even know this woman's name?" Virginia asked.

"I know her name, but she and her family don't know my name," Larry replied.

"I told you that this guy is gutsy," Scott said.

"No, the sister in prison is the gutsy one. She wasn't gonna' let some jerk ass destroy her sister. She didn't deserve to be in prison for having the guts to stop a monster," Larry said.

"Well, you have killed more people than anyone I ever heard of, so I'll take your word for it," Scott said.

"How many people have you killed?" Virginia asked.

"I couldn't give you an exact number, I'm afraid."

"When was the last time you killed someone?" she asked.

"The November before last, in Alexander Bay, New York. I killed two guys in scuba gear. It was around midnight. They knocked me into the water, so I had to kill them."

"I always thought that killing another person is morally indefensible," Virginia said.

"Well, it was dark, the water was ice cold and two guys knocked me into the water and were trying to kill me. I wasn't inclined to discuss any issues of morality at the time."

"That still doesn't change the moral indefensibility," she insisted.

"Is that what you think? Is that what you really think? Well, you're wrong!" Larry snapped.

Virginia looked at him for a moment then turned and walked away.

"You've really improved. Only one of them walked," Scott quipped.

"Ginny is a Quaker, but she'll get over it. What did you think about when you were killing those guys?" Montana asked.

"Killing them. It was a circumstance forced on me, so I just had to do it."

"No moral defense?" Dakota asked.

"The most common morally indefensible killing is abortion and liberal goofballs are almost always pro-abortion," Larry stated.

"That's very interesting. I've met a lot of military people, but none of them have talked about killing anybody. Maybe they didn't kill anybody or didn't want to talk about it," Dakota said.

"It's just part of the job."

"He sounds like Lieutenant Calley," Scott quipped.

"Who's Lieutenant Calley?" Montana asked.

"He did a 'road rage' act on a hundred and twenty civilians in Vietnam," Scott explained.

"He could have claimed that they were getting enemy fire and called up an artillery barrage or an airstrike. Fricking Army Lieutenant!"

"He wanted to be all that he could be."

"And that wasn't worth a shit, was it?" Larry asked rhetorically.

"It's just great listening to you guys. It's like being in a large bakery store and seeing all those goodies, but only able to take away a small part of them," Dakota remarked.

"Avoid the 'head up your ass' liberal mode and you can learn a lot," Larry said.

"Where are you guys staying," Montana asked.

"At the Sovereign," Scott replied.

"A guy was killed up there last month. On the fifth floor, I heard. Shot in the back with a .357 pistol while he slept. It was in the daytime, but nobody heard anything. There was nothing about it in the newspaper," she informed them.

"That doesn't sound good," Larry remarked.

"It could be drugs or smuggling, who knows. There is still a lot of that revolutionary stuff going on in the interior and on the east coast. It's quiet enough here usually. We stay around this part of the city. No touring the countryside," Dakota said.

"It was here or Kabul, I suppose," Larry quipped.

"You know it! Horrible weather in Kabul. We got a decent beach here, 365," Dakota said.

"You can't beat that."

"I've done some snorkeling, but I've been told that everything is either poisonous or will eat you. Sometimes there's sharks out there like you wouldn't believe and jellyfish too. Everybody says to stay in three feet or less," Montana informed them.

"You have a decent pool so leave the ocean to Larry," Scott said.

In another hour, most of the guests had left. Putzer had left a message for Larry to stay after the reception. Larry told the butler that he didn't feel like waiting around for Putzer or anybody else. He saw Barber and another fellow that looked like a native, go through another door. The

Butler returned and told Larry that the Envoy would see him now. Larry didn't ask to see the bastard so he figured he would tell him so. The butler took him to an office and rang the bell.

"Mister Mayer is here."

"Send him in," a voice said.

He opened the door and motioned for Larry to enter then he closed the door. Larry saw a man in the usual 'Black Tie' get-up, standing in front of the desk, looking at him like he was a worm.

"We haven't had a chance to meet, Mister Mayer."

"It is customary for the host to meet the guests when they arrive at a welcoming reception."

"I have been and am very busy," Putzer said.

"If you wanted to see me, make time."

"I have been looking at the reports..."

"Don't bother with reports from people who never dived in their life," Larry snapped.

Putzer looked at him for a moment.

"A lot of people are unhappy with your trial dives. They haven't been very impressive," he stated.

This asshole couldn't dive to the bottom of a kiddy pool and he's attacking my ability. He had no doubt that the useless lackey was bad mouthing him every chance he got. He's nothing but a pretty boy PR man. A cocktail party game playing son-of-a-bitch, Larry thought.

"That's what trial dives are for. I'm happy with the equipment and the people we got now. We should be able to get this done in one shot. I'm looking at the night after tomorrow. That'll give us three days to spare," Larry said as he went into a slow burn.

"I'm not sure that I can work with you."

Larry grabbed his tie and gave it a real hard jerk, throwing him to his knees.

"Last time, asshole, you ain't doing any work here. You're not diving and you won't even be there. Play your politics bullshit somewhere else. I'm not interested in you or your fucking reports or what your damn boss thinks. We are done here," Larry snapped.

Putzer got up and looked daggers at him as he left. General Barber met him outside the front entrance.

"How's things going, Chief?"

"Good, real good. We tested the 'Grab' last night. We used the 'dummy fish' filled with sand. I had no problem maneuvering it and getting it on at a thousand feet. That was a lift of a ton and a half," Larry informed him.

"Great, the hydrophone worked okay?"

"Yes, there was no problem with that."

"You're going out tomorrow night?" the general asked.

"Yes, there's no use pushing the guys. Give them a day to rest."

"When we get out there, you're gonna' attempt this in one shot?"

"Yes, I should be able to stay down long enough to get this done. The storage cylinders have been modified so that they can be drained and purged while containing the bombs," Larry said.

"Good, it sounds like you're as ready as you can be," the general said.

"As always, keep everybody away. Especially that asshole Putzer."

"I'm flying back with you guys in the morning. I have a car waiting to take you to the hotel," Barber said.

"Super."

"A vehicle will be waiting at 0900. It will take us straight to the airport."

"Great, that gives me plenty of time to sleep," Larry said.

He hadn't been in his room very long when he heard someone softly knocking on his door. When he opened the door, the young lady, Montana, was standing there.

"Hi again. I hope this isn't a bad time," she said.

"As good as any," Larry said as he motioned for her to come in.

"How did you know I was here?"

"Our housekeeper is a sister of the guy that manages this place," Montana replied.

"I see. What's on your mind?"

"I tried scuba diving in Florida with my sorority. I wasn't properly instructed though. There are a lot of good places to dive on this island. I was wondering if you were free anytime to go diving?"

"I'm afraid that we're pulling out early in the morning. I haven't been told about any plans to come back here later," Larry replied.

"That's too bad. Are you alone tonight?"

"I have a wife and a seven month old baby at home, I'm afraid."

"Oh, I didn't know! I'm sorry!"

"My fault. I didn't mention it earlier."

"I must be going..."

"Nice seeing you again. If you're ever on Nantucket, look me up. You can be our guest," Larry said.

"That's very kind of you."

"Not at all. We would love having you visit," Larry said.

After Montana left, he read for a while then he went to bed. Her mentioning that her housekeeper's brother runs the hotel is probably how she found out about the guy upstairs, getting killed. There was no telling if that had anything to do with this operation, but it seemed to cast another pall on things. The chambermaids banging things in the hallway, woke him up at seven o'clock. He got dressed and went downstairs. He ran into Scott and Barber and another guy in the dining room.

"You old son of a sea cook, sit right down here. George, this is Larry Mayer. He can dive all night or screw all night as the mood strikes him," Scott said.

They shook hands.

"Montana was just there a few minutes," Larry said as he sat down.

"Where?" Scott asked.

"My room. She was asking about doing some diving here and in Florida."

"You got young babes coming to your room and being a married man yet. Holy cow, Mayer the player here!"

"Just coffee," Larry told the waitress.

"I suppose you don't want to sleep too much at night."

"George here has met President Obama. Shook his hand and everything," Scott said.

"God, I would throw up if I was that close to that asshole," Larry said.

"We wouldn't want Larry's hands that close to Obama's neck," Scott joked.

"You say that everything he says is a lie. Can you explain?"

"In his campaign he swore that he was going to close Gitmo-he hasn't. He said that he was gonna' immediately stop the Patriot Act. He has renewed it and expanded it. He said that he was gonna' withdraw our troops from Iraq-he hasn't. He said that NAFTA was another Bush tax break for the wealthy when he wholeheartedly supported NAFTA. He said that he was gonna' reduce the budget deficit. I could go on and on but anybody who has half a brain can see that everything he says is a lie."

"How about Bush?"

"Bush very seldom lied. Every time I ask a brainless liberal when he lied, they always tell me it was about the WMD in Iraq. Newsflash! Congress had oversight here. Bush went to congress with the information he had and congress approved the war. The only people that continually lie are the liberals. Everytime they try to argue with me, I catch them in their lie almost immediately, then they try to shift the argument and I won't let them until they admit their lies then they go away mad," Larry concluded.

"Larry has a lot of bad republican friends and no democrat friends," Scott quipped.

"I'll let the president know the next time I see him," Barber said.

"Putzer didn't like my diving. Lacking any subtlety, he stated that my diving wasn't for shit," Larry said.

"And he still has his head!" Scott exclaimed.

"Technically he is just an accomadation address. He has no part in this operation, so his opinion doesn't mean anything," Barber said.

He had a report on the trial dives, Larry thought.

"He's a suck for somebody's dick," Larry snapped.

George began laughing at that.

"Maybe you should have given Montana a little more time," Scott quipped.

"I'm sure Shirley will be thrilled as it is."

After breakfast, they got their bags and took jeeps to the airport. A few more people that General Barber knew, but didn't bother to introduce, arrived about the same time that they did and they all got on the plane and it took off. While they were airborne, the copilot came back and informed them that there was some shooting outside of Trincomalee, but the pilot got clearance to land without a delay. Larry read a magazine until they landed. They would go aboard the ship, but the ship wouldn't leave the dock until shortly before sunset. More jeeps were there to take everyone to the Marine Challenger.

CHAPTER FOUR

On board the ship, one of the men who came with them from Columbo, was introduced as Hiram Beltz, an armorer specialist for nuclear weapons. He opened up a brief case and took out a diagram of the location of the electronics in a Mark 28 type thermo-nuclear bomb. He had a simplified diagram of the interlocks and he explained how they worked and in what sequence they had to be closed. He showed them only one diagram at a time then put them back into the briefcase. He took out a metal object about two inches wide, eight inches long and four inches high. He called it a Radio Altitude Detonator or RAD. It was held by four bolts, which had to be removed before the device could be removed from the bomb. An easy enough job on top, but Larry had doubts about doing it on the bottom. Barber showed him a socket wrench which had a fixture welded on that could be held by the claw on his suit. It would be installed before he went down. Larry was familiar with ham-fisted people who habitually overtightened bolts. According to Beltz, the bolts were at seventy five foot-pounds torque. Nothing was said about sea water getting into the bombs or whether any of the interlocks were closed. It seemed to Larry that if the bombs weren't on an airplane then none of the interlocks should be closed and he expressed that. Beltz replied that he honestly did not know for sure. Larry said that if the detonating charges did not explode when the bombs hit the water then the bombs should not be capable of exploding now. Beltz agreed that that should be the case. Well, he would be the first to find out otherwise, Larry thought.

After the specialists left, they had the usual briefing about the dive. Commander Holscomb and General Barber conducted the briefing, but all they really had to add was magnetic images of the bombs or what they thought were bombs. They could be water tanks lying on the bottom. There were no images or any other information about the conditions on the bottom. At this depth, Larry really didn't like this lack of information, but he could always abort the dive if necessary.

It was fully dark when the Marine Challenger came to a stop. As before, they lowered the RRV and got pictures of the bombs and their precise location on the sea floor. From the images, the objects looked like bombs and they seemed to be sitting on a solid sea floor. This time the RRV would stay down while Larry was lowered to the bottom. The system checks and the suiting up took forty minutes as before. The last thing his crew did was to attach the socket wrench to the left claw. It seemed that everybody was on deck to see him off. Everything went smoothly and it took twenty minutes to lower him to the bottom.

"On the bottom. I'm about twenty feet away. I'm using the MPU," Larry said.

"Roger that," Scott said.

The propulsion unit lifted him up slightly and pushed him ahead slowly until he was at the first bomb. He only had to bend over about thirty degrees in order to get the wrench on the bolt head.

"Attempting the first bolt on the RAD," Larry said.

"Roger that."

Larry tried using the wrench for a couple minutes, but to no avail.

"I can't get the bolts loose. I'll have to send it up with the RAD."

"Roger that, Chief."

"Standby to move the RRV."

"Roger that. Standing by, Chief."

"Move left."

"Move left, aye."

Larry could hear the directional propellers whining as the RRV moved for a minute.

"Stop left. Start Forward," he requested.

"Stop left, Start forward, aye."

For a minute, the RRV moved toward him.

"Stop forward."

"Stop Forward, aye," Scott acknowledged.

The RRV was about ten degrees off on the alignment but Larry would try to move it as it lowered.

"Steady as she goes, lower," Larry requested.

"Roger Chief, lowering."

Pushing with both arms, in a minute it was positioned on the bomb just like in the practice runs.

"Stop lowering."

"Roger that."

After the recovery vehicle stopped, Larry looked at it again to make sure it was positioned exactly right.

"Engage the grab," he requested.

There was a hesitation.

"Repeat the last transmission," another voice said.

"Engage the grab," Larry repeated.

"Roger that, engaging the grab," Scott said.

The four jaws slowly closed on the bomb, lifting it an inch or so in the process. Larry hooked the safety bar so that the grab couldn't be inadvertently opened on the way up. He stepped away from the Recovery Pod.

"Safety bar on. Raise it a couple feet," Larry requested.

"Roger that, stand clear."

When it was raised, he looked underneath to make sure that everything looked good. He installed an extra piece of equipment.

"Alright, take it up," he ordered.

"Roger that. Raising the Recovery Vehicle."

"Let me know when you got it on deck."

"Will do, Chief."

It took much longer than he thought.

"First package on deck ....What's with the damn padlock?"

"To help secure the safety bar. Albert has the keys," Larry replied.

"Roger that," Scott acknowledged.

It took forty minutes to get the bomb secured and another forty minutes to lower the RRV. Larry told them how the other bomb was laying relative to the first so they could move the crane around. The RAD wasn't even visible so Larry made no attempt to remove it. He had them stop the RRV just five feet above the bomb.

"Move right."

"Move right, aye."

In less than a minute it was in position.

"Stop right. Steady as she goes, lower."

"Steady as she goes, lower, aye."

The RRV came down right over the bomb.

"Stop lowering and engage grab."

"Stop lowering and engage grab, aye."

He watched the jaws of the grab as they closed around the bomb. Everything looked good so he decided to make a little game change. He set the propulsion unit to vertical and moved up the side of the RRV until he could grasp a cable and get his feet on the frame. He seemed to be secure enough he thought.

"Alright, raise the RRV," he requested.

"Raise the RRV, aye."

Larry rode the recovery vehicle as the bomb was hoisted up. At one hundred feet, the recovery vehicle stopped. Larry looked around and saw a diver with a knife, coming at him, just a couple feet away, in the darkness. He knew that a diver's knife was useless against his hardsuit. He opened the claw on the left and grabbed at his regulator line. The diver tried to back away while Larry pulled the other way, ripping the line out and pulling the regulator from his mouth. He had an octopus regulator, so he beat a hasty retreat. A second diver tried to tackle him and wrestle him away from the RRV, so he grabbed at his crotch with the other claw. The diver struggled to get away, but Larry was determined to land this fish. He slammed him on the side of his head with the left claw. He hit him several more times then he grabbed his first stage regulator with the claw and locked it from inside. This way he could hold the diver away from him. After another five minutes, the recovery vehicle began to rise again. When it broke the surface, someone stopped raising it. Larry signaled to continue raising. If there was a problem, they could solve it just as easily on deck, he figured. After a minute, the recovery vehicle began rising again. When it was high enough, it was swung over and lowered onto the cradle for the bomb. When the bomb was released, the recovery vehicle was swung over and lowered onto the deck. Several men grabbed the scuba diver, so Larry released the claw. Since the suit weighed more than six hundred pounds, Larry had to wait until the deck crew could get the line reeled in and lower him to the deck. It took a few minutes to get his faceplate off. General Barber was among the men standing around him.

"How do you feel, Chief?" Commander Holscomb asked.

"I'm fine, how's you?" Larry quipped.

"We'll get you outta' here and to sick bay in just a minute."

"I don't need no sick bay, Commander," Larry said.

"It's just routine."

"The routine medicals were always done out here on deck. What did you do with the other guy?"

"What other guy?"

"The guy I brought up with me, Commander."

"I was here the whole time. I didn't see anybody else come up with you." he stated.

"Then you're a mother fucking liar," Larry snapped.

"I'm the commander of this vessel, Mayer," he snapped.

"And you're still a liar."

"I'll see you in my quarters when you're done here," he said then he turned and walked away.

The tenders removed the head portion of the suit then loosened it at the waist and removed the upper half of the shell. Albert and Dale helped lift him out of the lower portion, and they set him on the deck.

"Thanks guys," Larry said.

He went to the recovery vehicle. In the netting between the framework and the machinery, he found the diver's regulator with the broken hose still attached. He picked it up and put it in the pocket of his coveralls.

"Somebody lose some gear there," Hal said, smiling.

"You know they did."

"In these Spook operations, you don't say anything, ever."

Ashore, but during the operation, I'm gonna' ask questions," Larry said.

Larry didn't wait for the doctor's examination. He went right to the Commander's quarters. When he got there, General Barber was there.

"You look like you could use a cup of coffee."

"Cut the crap," Larry demanded.

"We haven't been quite up front with you. As you know, the hard part of making nuclear weapons is to make enough fissionable material of weapons grade. One country in particular has been trying to get their nukes surreptitiously. This was supposed to be an unsuccessful operation to recover two nuclear packages. The bombs in question are quite conventional in fact. They contain electronic equipment that enable them to be tracked underwater or underground. Unfortunately, you kinda' balled up that plan, Chief."

"Fucking god damn cowboy! Captain America here just blew a very costly operation. We finally got a door open to these people and you blew it all to hell!" Commander Holscomb said as he came in.

"You gotta' be fucking kidding me. Nobody is gonna' believe that bombs got lost while be hoisted to the surface. Even the Steelers wouldn't try that fucking play," Larry said.

"The Chief is right. The ruse of stopping at a hundred feet may have looked too obvious, but with one diver driven off and the other one killed, it looks like something worth dying for. You killed Escencio, by the way," Barber informed him.

"He didn't have the good sense to back off. How did you know his name?"

"He had a tattoo with his name and Serena."

"Always include where to send the flowers," Larry quipped.

"You think this is funny!" Holscomb snapped.

"I've had worse moments, Commander," he replied.

"We'll see about that. We're going to Bangkok."

"Sorry, I'm not an 'on the ground type'. I did the wet work, now I'm shoving off here."

"Hillary is coming. You definitely don't want to miss her."

"I definitely do, I'm afraid," Larry said.

As the Marine Challenger got underway, Barber sent a message-'Butcher, Baker and Candlestick maker."

The reply-'Little Bo Peep lost her Sheep?"

"Negative, repeat, negative," Barber sent.

"Stand by, will advise."

CHAPTER FIVE

The Marine Challenger sailed around Sri Lanka and docked at Columbo. Larry and Barber got on a plane that took them to Bangkok. After getting him a room at the Royal Siam, Barber instructed Larry to go to the bar next door and wait for him. They wanted an anchorman so everyone didn't enter the bar together and at the same time. Larry found a table and ordered the plum wine and ignored it while he waited. From what he could see, there were only Chinese and Thais in the place. It wasn't long before another white man came to his table.

"Do you mind if I join you?" he asked with an Australian accent.

"Not at all," Larry replied.

"Thanks, Mate. I was wanting to sit with someone that speaks English."

"Not too many choices here, I'm afraid," Larry said.

"Martin Howard," he said, holding out his hand.

"Larry Mayer," Larry said as they shook hands.

"You're an American? I'm from Victoria," he said.

"Pleased to meet you."

"Can I get you a drink?"

"This one should be enough, but thank you anyways," Larry said.

"Are you meeting someone here?"

"I'm supposed to. They frequently get distracted and don't show up."

"Yeah, I know about that. Our company sells things to militaries around the world. Everything, but weapons. We do a lot of our business here. What happens here, stays here as you chaps say. A lot of Chinese come here. We get them pissed and get women to ride their brains out. They expect to get that kind of thing before they talk business," Martin explained.

"There are worse jobs, I suppose," Larry said smiling.

"What's your line of work?"

"Deep sea diving."

"Really, what shill is that?"

"Marine Challenger," Larry replied, giving them the name of the vessel instead of a fake company.

"Never heard of them," he said.

"It's a full service diving company. Oil rigs take up a lot of our time. Right now we're doing some deep water diving for Television outfits. They pretend like it is their equipment and divers when it's shown on TV," Larry explained.

"How deep were you diving?"

"We went to two thousand feet. That was east of Sri Lanka."

"Bloody hell, you say! What's down there?"

"Nothing. The deeper you dive, the less there is to see. You don't know what a pain it is to stir up something worth filming."

"There's nothing down there that wants you messing with it," Martin said.

"Yeah, It's a good bet that everything we run into has never seen a diver before."

"How much does it cost for a days work?" Martin asked.

"It's a $120,000 day for the ship. I don't know what else it costs. They don't pay us tremendously, that's for sure," Larry said.

"I was reading that an American actor gets paid two hundred thousand dollars to make one episode of a television series."

"Renting our ship must sound like a bargain to that producer," Larry remarked.

"In Australia, we have a gun called the Steyr AUG. Are you familiar with that?" he asked.

"Oh yes," Larry said.

"What do you think of it?"

"I'm not a fan of plastic guns. It looks and feels like a toy," Larry said.

"It shoots well enough."

"Lousy trigger pull and the telescopic sight isn't adjustable."

"It is on later models," Martin corrected him.

"The Daewoo is the best thing in .223. It beats the hell outta' anything I've found."

"I could get you a commercial Steyr for a song. Brand new, in the box."

"I don't think I'll be carrying that around in my suitcase," Larry quipped.

"Keep me in mind if you need one."

"I will," Larry said, wondering if he would need that much firepower.

"Do you think your mates would be interested in any of our wares?"

"The skipper and the producer don't know one end of a gun from the other. I don't know who else they're bringing. If you work the military outfits, this is hardly your thing. You expect to sell a hundred thousand things at a time. I don't know anybody who buys like that," Larry said.

After the Australian left, a waiter brought him a note from Barber to return to the hotel.

A white man in a white suit, climbed the stairs to a non-air conditioned office above a sheet metal warehouse in Bangkok. Two men in turbans, obviously Muslims, and an 'oriental' looking man in a white, short sleeve shirt were there to meet him.

"Mister Cole, I was afraid that you wouldn't come," the man said, but neither he, or the Muslims stood up.

"Chai, great seeing you again," the man, who strongly resembled Joe Cole, said as he shook hands with him.

"This is Sheik Watajah and Hasan Gaikwad."

"Nice meeting you, gentlemen," the white man said since they didn't stand up or offer their hand.

"These gentlemen were somewhat disappointed that the packages were not delivered."

"So I heard. You hired those two Portugese divers. One was driven off and the other was killed by the recovery diver," 'Joe' said.

"The diver reported that the first time, the safety bar had been secured by a heavy padlock. The second time, the diver came up with the recovery vehicle. He was very determined to protect those bombs. Our information is that the man's name is Larry Mayer."

"Hmm, that sounds familiar. He must have been a Navy guy," the 'Joe' said.

"I should think that is quite likely. Quite likely that the United States Navy doesn't want to lose those bombs again," Chai stated, adding-"As these gentlemen have pointed out, quite a bit of money has been invested already."

"Yes, I appreciate that. The divers failed to obtain the bombs. I arranged for the Recovery Vehicle to be held at a hundred feet for ten minutes and no other divers in the water except for the recovery diver. Obviously this was just an honest miss."

"This has 'queered the pitch' as you say, for any more attempts. Not so?" Chai said.

"Not necessarily. The bombs aren't on a navy vessel as yet," the 'Joe' said.

"Are you certain that the sea water has not destroyed the bombs?"

"There should be little or no damage to the internal components. If your people are knowledgeable and have the facilities you say, there should be no problem with dismantling the bombs and making any repairs necessary," the 'Joe' said.

The next night, Larry was sitting in the same lounge and at the same table, with General Barber and an Attache' or Secretary of something- General Wilkins. Larry had been briefed earlier and seen a transcript of the conversation that was supposed to take place. There was a belief that the arms 'dealers' had somebody who spoke English and could read lips as well. The two Vietnamese nationals would not show up until Barber and Wilkins had left. Larry felt apprehensive but maybe that would play into their game since he had never met the arms buyers.

"Hello, Tony," Larry said as they shook hands.

"Do you know Cal Wilkins?" Barber asked.

"By reputation, of course. Nice to meet you," Larry said as they shook hands then they sat down.

"I have arranged for the transportation. This is a civilian ship, so you have to arrange for the drop. Civilian means that it could be stopped by any navy or customs vessel out there. The ship has to dock and make the drop quickly. You'll have to be there. We don't want to be anywhere around," Barber said.

"I'll go to 'Nam and make the contacts. I'm sure that there will be no problems. They want those packages delivered," Larry said.

"Cal will be in contact at the other end."

"I understand that you have an unregistered C-130 to fly to Pakistan. We have it handled on our end. Have you considered that Coalition aerial surveillance will pick up anything flying over Afghanistan, Iraq or Iran," Larry said.

"Yes, they'll probably have to move the packages by truck. They're only about two tons apiece, so they can come up with that part," Cal said.

"It sounds like more time and more money will be required," Barber said.

"More time, but not more money. We gotta' deal with these people in good faith. We can't start that kind of talk on the first deal. Everybody will have to take their percentage and be happy for now," Larry stated.

"Governments, including ours, give rewards for this kind of thing. Some of our friends might get unhappy and squeal," Wilkins said.

"All of my associates know better than that. If you have any doubts about your guys then you better deal with them, pronto," Larry snapped.

"That won't be necessary, Larry. You must remember that we've already done ninety percent of the work. When you and your friends do the rest, everybody will be happy," Barber said.

"That's good. I don't want to look like a monkey's ass to anybody. When I'm waiting at that dock, the Maritime Challenger comes in and not a guided missile cruiser," Larry said.

"Yes, everything will go as planned. You handle things at the unloading. You're turning red. I don't like a guy that gets excited," Barber said.

"Right, let's not get excited here," Larry said as he relaxed and sat back in the chair. He hoped that his act was convincing to any watchers.

"You keep in touch. You know how to reach us," Barber said as they all stood up.

"Certainly, nice seeing you again," Larry said as they shook hands.

After Barber and Wilkins left, Larry sat down and drank, or pretended to drink his beer. A few minutes later, two oriental men looked to be passing by then suddenly stopped.

"Mister Mayer?"

Larry stood up.

"I am Ben-Doh and this is Mister Tung."

Ben-Doh had the typical Chinese businessman look while Tung was taller and had a more Mongolian face.

"Nice to meet you," Larry said as he shook hands with them.

"Please sit," Larry said, indicating the chairs.

"Thank you," Ben-Doh said.

"Would you like something to drink?"

"No, we are fine."

"Chai said that you are the transportation specialists in Vietnam."

"Yes, we can deliver packages just about anywhere," Ben-Doh said.

"Good, two crates, about two tons each, will be on the deck of a ship. The ship will dock in Cam Ranh Bay. I don't know when yet. The crates will be lifted off by a crane and set on your trucks. Your trucks will take them to a location in the countryside. I have been assured that there will be no problem with police or soldiers, but your trucks must be at the dock on time and must deliver the packages on time. The schedule allows sufficient time to get to the destination. As you know, these packages are valuable and cannot be lost or damaged. Chai told me that you are the people to handle this sort of thing."

"Yes, we can handle this delivery, Mister Mayer," Ben-Doh said.

"Do you need to discuss this with Tung?"

"I speak English, Mister Mayer," Tung informed him.

"Oh, I'm sorry. You're being so quiet," Larry said, smiling.

"Here is my card. My phone operator speaks English. When your ship is coming in, give me a call and my trucks will be there," Ben-Doh said.

"Excellent," Larry replied.

"Have you seen the shows and the gambling?" Tung asked.

"No, I didn't know they had such a thing," Larry said.

"We will show you, if you like?"

"Very well," Larry said, but he wasn't sure what he was getting into.

They went back to the kitchen and Ben'Doh said something to somebody in a suit then they followed him up a stairs. The man opened a door with a key and they entered a rather dingy hallway that smelled of opium smoke. Going down the hallway, they went through a door at the end and entered what looked like a seedy lounge. Ben-Doh and Tung talked to a man then pointed at Larry and talked some more then were led to a table.

"Just about anything you want can be had here," Tung said as they sat down.

Larry was afraid to drink or eat anything. He was afraid that he might slip up and say something that betrayed him. A waiter came over.

"He wants to know if you want something to drink?" Tung said.

"Uh, maybe later," Larry said.

"Come on, I'm buying," Tung said.

"Alright, a martini"

"Three," Tung said, and the waiter nodded and left.

"I know that these places have a bad reputation in the West, but I assure you that you are perfectly safe. Please try to relax and enjoy yourself," Ben-Doh said.

"Thank you," Larry said.

A young lady, no more than sixteen, was singing a song in Thai, which of course meant nothing to Larry.

"They switch languages. Soon she will sing in English," Tung assured him as the waitress came with the drinks.

The next song she sang was the Butterfly Opera and she did a good job, Larry thought. After doing a song in Chinese, she left the stage.

"The Burlesque show will start," Ben-Doh said.

"You'll like this," Tung assured him.

After a minute of traditional music, the spotlight came on and a young woman, probably twenty or twenty one, came out in the sarong type dress and began to gyrate around in unusual ways. Some men were taking pictures with their cellphones. She danced from one end of the stage to the other, dropping portions of her garment as she went. When she got back to the middle, she was wearing only an undergarment composed of strings of beads. This hardly covered her womanly charms as she danced and then rolled around on the stage. Tung went down to get a closer look.

"What do you think of that show?" Ben-Doh asked.

"Where I come from, the state has outlawed nude dancing, I'm afraid," Larry informed him.

"Here, just about everything is allowed. People know to behave themselves and not start trouble, you see," he explained.

"Glad to hear it. I wouldn't want a fight to start."

Tung came back.

"I would like to eat that for supper," he said, smiling.

"You never know where that's been," Larry said.

"There are girls here if you want one," Ben-Doh said.

"I have a girl back home," Larry said.

"Not like these," Tung said.

Another girl came out and danced and a man came out and they stripped each other while dancing. After that a woman came out and danced and a man came out and had sex with her and another man came out for a threesome. The acts continued in their debauchery until they had done practically everything men and women can do. After the fifth act, Larry said that he was tired, so Ben-Doh had a busboy escort him back to his hotel. Barber was waiting for him when he came in. He had come through the unused connecting doorway, so he didn't have to use the hallway where he could be seen.

"How did it go?"

"They agreed to pick up the crates."

"Great, everything is all set then. Where were you?"

"They took me to one of the local dives."

"I hope you didn't drink anything that I wouldn't drink?"

"I dumped most of it on the floor."

"Good man. We'll go to Vietnam tomorrow. It's a two hour flight," Barber said.

"Not too early."

"Good night," Barber said then he left.

The only flight to Ho Chi Minh City was 0600 the next morning. Barber was supposed to be on the plane with Larry, but he had to cancel at the last minute. Larry had been given a cover story about looking for a location for a start-up business in sheet metal stamping. Of course, there was some machinery arriving in crates later on and customs had been informed that it would be warehoused until a production plant site was chosen. The man who would see to it that the police and the government would stay away was named Bo Pon. Ben-Doh had made the introduction by telephone and sent a picture by fax. Larry was assured that Bo would send an employee to pick him up at the airport.

CHAPTER SIX

"Hello, Mister Mayer. Have you been in our country before?" Bo Pon asked.

"Only for a brief time in '75," Larry replied.

"I see. Much has changed, but much has remained the same. The lower floor is still a house of love. Doubtless you saw the girls hanging the clothing out back?" he asked as they walked up the steps.

"Yes, I did."

"There is still a good atmosphere here. That is how you say it?"

"Yes, that is correct."

They went through a door and down a hallway. They went through a steel security door and into a short hallway in front of his office. Larry was surprised to see TV monitors.

"As you can see, this is new. Before this we sent an old woman around to make sure that there were no problems. Almost always, everyone is very well behaved," he explained as he stopped and pointed at a monitor.

Larry saw a naked Vietnamese girl sitting on a man who looked like Joe Cole. She was moving her pelvis forward and back slowly while she talked softly. When Vietnamese women talk softly, it sounds like they're singing a lullaby.

"You can, of course, avail yourself of any of the services," he offered.

"Some other time perhaps," Larry said, hoping that Bo Pon thought the sex was what got his attention.

He opened his office door and motioned for Larry to go in then he closed the door.

"As you can see, I have a bar. I have grown accustomed to having a Bourbon and Branch water at this time in the afternoon. Would you like one?"

"Just a small one for now," Larry said, knowing that it would be difficult for his host to drink if he wasn't.

"Tung and Ben-Doh have been friends of mine for a long time."

"A barrel of laughs, those two," Larry said.

"Their humor may be hard to understand, but I assure you that they have always been impeccably correct in all their dealings."

"This is a somewhat different deal than usual. Twenty two inches in diameter, eight and a half feet long and two tons. There can't be any banging or dropping these packages."

"Are they hot?" Bo Pon asked.

"No, there is no radiation leak whatsoever. The shell is air tight. It must remain that way. The interior is an atmosphere of pure nitrogen and Argon. Otherwise, they are intrinsically safe. The interlocks are all 'fail to safe'. All you need is a technician that understands these things," Larry explained.

"Excellent, I will meet you in front of the Archipelago at four," Bo Pon said as he held out his hand.

"Great, let's get this done," Larry said enthusiastically as they shook hands.

As they went to a table, Larry caught the faint smell of smoke from raw opium. When they got to the table, the man he had seen on the monitor and another Chinese man stood up.

"Larry Mayer, this is Ho Van Ng ... and this is Joe Cole," Bo said as they shook hands.

"Nice meeting you," the 'Joe' said in an unfamiliar voice.

"You look vaguely familiar. Maybe from Boot Camp years ago."

"That could be. Where were you?" he asked.

"San Diego," Larry said.

"It couldn't have been there. I was at Great Lakes," he said.

"This just routine, of course, but since you're American, I need to see some ID," Larry said.

Neither of the other guys said anything as the 'Joe' took out his wallet. He showed him a California driver's license with Joe Cole's birth date and former address in Modesto. The date issued was before Joe had moved to the Virgin Islands. Joe had shown Larry his Virgin Islands license when he visited him.

"Oh, you're from Modesto. Scott Peterson was from there, wasn't he?"

"I understand that he was," the 'Joe' said as he put his wallet back in his pocket.

"I met a guy in New York who said that he played golf with him. Claimed that he cheated in the scoring. I never did care for anybody that cheated in Golf or Bridge," Larry said.

"I hope that Bo Pon has been treating you gentlemen well," Ho said.

"Very well. We have lacked for nothing," the 'Joe' said.

"I understand that the Jerusalem operation was derailed," Ho said.

"It's back on track, but there was an unavoidable delay," Larry said.

"I should hope that the delay will not be for long."

"Two or three days, no longer," Larry stated.

"How can you be so certain?" Ho asked.

"The packages will be crated up. We have arranged for identical crates to be fabricated. Our General on the inside will arrange for the wrong crates to be transferred to the USN sub tender then the Marine Challenger will proceed to Cam Ranh Bay for the transfer," Larry explained.

"This plan sounds rather sketchy."

"Of course, that is just an outline. The details have already been worked and the most difficult parts of the plan have already been completed with no problems," Larry said, trying to sound convincing.

"And no additional payments will be required?" Ho asked.

"Absolutely not. We have always dealt with our buyers in good faith," Larry assured him.

"That is good to hear, Mister Mayer."

"Mister Cole, you will handle the transfer on land?" Ho asked.

"Yes, once the ship arrives, flatbed trucks will be there and the crates will be immediately set on the trucks and secured. Everything is good on our end and the route is clear and secured by Bo and his friends, the Thais. All problems have been anticipated," the 'Joe' said.

"Excellent, my friends look forward to getting the packages delivered," Ho said.

They watched a tradition 'ballet' then they left. Ho walked out to the street with them.

"A three wheeler should come by soon. I will tell him to take you back to the docks," Ho said.

"Much obliged," Larry said.

"The streets are safe now at day or night. Not so when you were here," Ho said after a moment.

"That's free enterprise. Always somebody trying to get enterprising," Larry said.

"I was much younger in '75. When the People's Army came, they grabbed all of our group. Since I was only thirteen, they pounded the hell outta' me as I watched them shoot all my friends in the courtyard behind the old police station. I learned to operate with the permission of the government. The Chinese and the Russians came, so some services were required for them. I understand that keeping girls is not permitted in America."

"Where I come from, it is still illegal to be in bed with a woman you're not married to. Almost always this law is not enforced," Larry explained.

"It is unnatural to keep men and women apart, is it not?" Ho asked.

"I'm sure that most people think so," Larry replied.

"Of course, two men or two women together is quite a different matter. The penalties are quite severe, I'm afraid."

"I see that you folks know where to draw the line," Larry remarked.

The 'Joe' whistled very sharply.

"Oh, very good, Mister Cole," Ho said as a motorcycle cab came around the corner.

When he stopped in front of them, Larry and the 'Joe' shook Ho's hand then got in. Ho said something to the driver and gave him some money. The driver nodded his head and pulled away after Ho had stepped back.

"This guy doesn't understand a word we say," the 'Joe' said.

"Too bad, he looks like he could use a laugh tonight."

"Ho wouldn't be too amused to find out that the recovery diver was in fact you," the 'Joe' said.

"He would probably be a lot more perturbed to hear that you are not Joe Cole."

"Bullshit!"

"I have known Joe Cole for forty years. He died a year ago, November," Larry stated.

"It looks like we both better play along," he said after a minute.

"Uh, uh, Nuclear bombs are nothing to play with. I've had enough already. I'm pulling out."

"Ho and friends will be mighty disappointed if you do."

"Look, I'm not looking for anymore nukes sitting on the bottom of the ocean. I've gotten too deep in this deal and for nothing but trouble."

The 'Joe' tapped the driver on the left shoulder to indicate that he should turn left.

"I'm going back to Bo Pon's. I promised Li Ming that I would come back."

"I wouldn't go anywhere near there," Larry said.

After 'Joe' got off at the House of Love, Larry directed the driver to the hotel. Fortunately the driver recognized the name of the place. Larry wrote a note to the desk clerk and he waited outside while the driver went in. In a few minutes the driver returned with his suitcase. Larry signed for him to open it. The driver looked nervous, but he set it down on the street and released the latches while Larry kept a safe distance. He removed his clothes then Larry checked the inside for anything suspicious. Finding nothing, he signed for the driver to put everything back in. After the driver was done, he gave the suitcase to Larry along with a dirty look. Larry smiled at him and gave him twenty, one dollar bills. The driver looked to be in shock as he looked at it. Larry said the name of the airfield, and the driver nodded and motioned for him to get in.

When they got to the airfield, the driver took his bag from him and they went into the terminal together. Larry went to the only counter that was open. A pretty young Vietnamese woman in a white blouse and black skirt, no more than twenty years old, smiled at him. The driver rattled off quite a pronouncement in Vietnamese to her as Larry handed her his passport and his foreign business document. A piece of heavy yellow paper which had writing on both sides and not a word in English.

"You wish to return to Bangkok, Mister Mayer?"

"Yes, on any flight and as soon as possible," Larry said.

"I must ask the purpose of you leaving so soon."

"My wife is very close to having our child. I wish to be there," Larry explained.

"You do not look as a man having a family," she said as she looked at him strangely.

He reached into his pocket and pulled out the picture of him standing with Shirley. Her big baby belly was evident. Although this wasn't any sort of proof for him being in a hurry, he hoped that she would buy it.

"Very well. There is a 7 p.m. flight to Bangkok. It is all military people, but I can get you on it if you like."

"That will be quite acceptable. Thank you," Larry said as he handed her his charge card and his suitcase.

It took her about ten minutes to produce the ticket then she handed it to Larry. The driver spoke again.

"Nu will wait here with you. He doesn't want to go back because he has made his fares and he will waste gasoline that he doesn't want to pay for," she explained.

"That sounds like a good idea," Larry said then he smiled at Nu.

"If you need anything, let me know. You can call me Suzy," she said.

"Thank you very much. You have been most helpful," Larry said then they went to the nearest padded bench.

A few minutes later, a group of Army fellows came in. Mostly officers, their commander began talking to Suzy. Suzy pointed his way, and they all turned and looked at him. After a few minutes, the officers began sitting on the benches while their commander came over to Larry. Larry stood up.

"Good evening, I am La Ky," he said as he put out his hand.

"I am Larry Mayer," Larry said as they shook hands.

"You must leave the country in a hurry?" he asked.

"Yes, I received a telephone call that my wife may be having our baby sooner than expected."

"I see. I hope that there are no problems for her."

"Thank you. I hope so too."

"Miss Trong says that your wife is very beautiful," Ky remarked.

God, he's one of these guys that's got a thing for 'round-eyed' women, Larry thought as he took out the picture he showed Suzy and handed it to him. He looked at it for a minute then handed it to another officer and so on until all of them had seen it.

"Quite right, Mister Mayer. She very beautiful and very close to having the child."

"It's a little soon. I thought I would have plenty of time to get home."

"Were you ever in our country?" Ky asked.

"Back in 1975, for a short time."

"Were you fighting...uh, in combat?"

"No, I wasn't. We were taking a number of vessels out of the country. We ended up taking them to Subic Bay in the Phillipines," Larry explained.

"It is a shame that we were at war. We have tried to be friendly to Americans," he said.

"Yes, people have been very friendly and very helpful. I have been happy to be here," Larry said.

"Where do you live?"

"On Nantucket Island."

"Is that a good place?" Ky asked.

"I suppose. It was always my wife's home, so I moved there," Larry explained.

"If I make it to America, perhaps I could visit you."

"Certainly, it's not a big island. Anybody can tell you where I live. I would be happy to have you visit us," Larry said.

"Are all the women pretty like your wife?"

There you go, Horn Dog, Larry thought.

"Yes, all the women are like that."

"My wife died last year, so I am 'Looking' as you say," Ky explained.

"Certainly. My wife died several years ago. Shirley has been everything to me."

"Doubtless that is why you are very anxious to return to her."

"Yes, I am very anxious to see her again, for sure," Larry said.

Very anxious to get outta' this damn place before any number of pissed-off people find me, Larry thought.

The driver said something to him.

"He asks if you wish some rice and fish," Ky said.

"No, but I'll spring for his," Larry said, taking a dollar out of his pocket and handing it to him.

Ky said something to him then the driver left.

"We have a sea animal, I can't think what you call it," he said as he did the crawling spider with his hand.

"A shrimp?" Larry asked.

"Yes, the mud shrimp. Most Americans will not eat it."

"Unfortunately it didn't look very well cooked," Larry said.

"Americans eat oysters uncooked, not so?"

"Yes, some people will, but I won't. Those things live in the mud on the bottom and they suck in that mud all the time. I'm not eating anything like that, cooked or not."

It wasn't long before the announcement in Vietnamese that their plane was ready to board. The Commander insisted that Larry sit at the front with him. Fortunately he let Larry sleep during the two hour flight. When the aircraft landed in Bangkok, the commander introduced him to his Thai counterpart. Larry politely turned down an invitation to join them for a night on the town. Using an airport courtesy phone, he called General Wilkins immediately and told him that he wanted to meet with General Barber ASAP. Wilkins said that he would pass on the message. At ten o'clock, he was picked up by a van. It was an operations van made to look like an ordinary civilian vehicle. He got in the back and Barber closed the security door.

"That was quick," he remarked.

"I ran into a guy that looked like Joe Cole. He had Joe's California driver's license and he didn't know me from Adam," Larry stated.

"That's interesting. At least you weren't seeing a ghost."

"He told me that he knew I was the recovery diver on the Challenger. Apparently someone told him who the recovery diver was before Bo Pon introduced us. Fortunately he didn't say anything in front of the Dinks. I told him that I would tell them that he isn't Joe Cole. He told me that I was crazy, but I told him that I had known Joe Cole for forty years. He said that he would not say anything about me."

"That's very interesting. What was he wearing?"

"A white suit."

"When did you first see him?"

"At 1200 hours, on a TV monitor at Bo Pon's House of Love. He was under one of the working girls," Larry replied.

"Where did you see him last?"

"Sometime before 1900. We took the same three-wheeler from Ho Van Ng's place. He got off in front of Bo's place. I told him that I wouldn't go back there," Larry replied.

"Interesting. Our embassy was just informed that a man, believed to be an American, 5'10" tall, dark hair, wearing a white jacket and slacks and having no identification or anything else on him, was just found floating near a pier. He was stabbed multiple times, according to the River Police," Barber said.

"That certainly didn't take them long. This 'Joe' was telling the Dinks how he arranged for the RRV to be stopped for ten minutes at a hundred feet. He knew that the recovery diver was the only person in the water. Apparently the Portugese divers weren't his responsibility, according to him. Ho didn't look placated in the least. They mentioned that considerable money had been spent in this operation and that the pitch had been queered for any save attempt. When it was time to leave, I figured that meant the country," Larry said.

"Yes, it's too bad that we don't have more to go on."

"You got five names. Give them to the Cultural Guards and let them kill some miserable bastards," Larry said.

"We don't have any evidence and we're not sending you back."

"No damn way I'm going back. I'd bet my ass that Ho and company are trying to take out both of us. We're just loose ends of a failed operation."

"We'll get you some food and a hotel. Stay in your room and do not leave for any reason. You will receive a phone call, but I cannot tell you when. The person will identify himself as Samson. You will receive instructions on where to go and what to do. Any questions?"

"Yeah, a lot of people have been getting killed here. I will need a firearm," Larry insisted.

"I have a Mark 3 pistol here. You can put it in your bag," Barber said.

He opened a drawer and took out the pistol. He also handed Larry some .22 rounds in a small box. Larry saw it that it had the larger and better CIA SAK suppressor. He removed the magazine and opened the action to check the chamber. He inserted the magazine and chambered a round.

"What's in that box?" Larry asked.

"Work gloves," Barber answered.

Larry pointed the gun at the box and pulled the trigger. He heard the click of the firing pin and the thud as the bullet penetrated the box and its contents.

"Just testing," Larry said in response to the dirty look he received.

CHAPTER SEVEN

It was after eleven when the phone rang in his room.

"Hello."

There was no voice, just breathing at the other end then it went dead. He went to his suitcase and removed the Ruger pistol. He fired it into a phone book to make sure it worked. It's time to go on the offensive, he thought. He turned off the light in his room before opening the door with his right foot. He heard the unmistakable sound of a cat squalling in the dark hallway. The room was at the end of the hall, so they had to be coming from the left. He shoved the door open rapidly and turned on the flashlight. He saw three young Thais in t-shirts, immediately opening their butterfly knives. No time for discussion here, Larry thought as he lined up on the oldest and largest one in the middle. In hardly more than a second, there were three clicks and three forty grain bullets in his chest. Not very impressive since his companions came on faster. He locked onto the one on the left and fired four rounds in two seconds. Not a lot of hitting power and not a lot of time, he knew as he aimed at last guy and put his final round into his forehead from five feet away. He fell right in front of him. Larry watched his losing struggle with death for a moment. He was no more than seventeen or eighteen. A young thug for hire. A guy that had no reason to bear any malice toward him. For a moment he thought about Althea never seeing him again. He gave the punk a good hard stomp on the temple to speed him on his way. He went into his room and reloaded the magazine then put the pistol in his suitcase. He left the room key on the nightstand and left the room. When he got downstairs, the guy at the desk didn't even look his way and he hoped to leave the building unobserved. Once outside, he quickly looked around to see if Kooklah, Fran and Capone had any friends waiting out there. A policeman had pulled over a car right in front of the door and was searching it. That might help, Larry thought as he began looking for a cab. In just a moment, he saw a cab going the other way. He whistled and held up his hand. Even that late at night, the traffic was heavy and Larry thought that the driver would keep going. The cabbies timing left nothing to be desired as he started his left turn between the two cars in the left lane. Crossing the centerline, he just missed a car, passing behind it then he cut across the next three lanes to complete his U-turn, ending up in front of the police car. The policeman gave the cabbie a dirty look as Larry went out into the street and opened the door and got in. He said 'American Consulate' and said the name of the street in Thai. The driver nodded his head and pulled away.

At the embassy, Larry had to surrender his pistol at the front desk to an assistant to 'somebody' from the State Department. He asked Larry where he got the pistol, so he told him it was General Barber. Larry cautioned him about being able to answer questions. Everybody who was anybody had already gone home, so Larry expected that he would have to sleep on a bench. Eventually a short fellow, no more than 5'4", in a beach robe, came up to him and he stood.

"I'm Fabian Smythe, the Charge de' Affaires," he said as he held out his hand.

"Larry Mayer," Larry said as they shook hands.

"We usually don't get called out at this hour. Why are you here?"

"Running for my life you might say."

"Do tell. I'll have the Resident Envoy take a statement then we can all get some sleep. I'll see you around nine o'clock," Smythe said.

"Certainly and thank you," Larry said.

In a few minutes, a man, about forty, came in with a woman about fifty. He introduced himself only as the Resident Envoy and the woman as his secretary. Larry informed the Resident Envoy that he didn't know how much information he could divulge. He told him about meeting General Barber earlier that night and the three punks in the hallway with knives and giving the pistol to somebody at a desk, from the State Department. The Resident Envoy showed no emotion or said anything to either of them until that time.

"Are you telling me that you entered by the front gate with a firearm in your possession?"

"Yes, a Mark 3 pistol is a firearm, though not very impressive, I admit," Larry answered.

The Envoy picked up the phone and called somebody like it was a dire emergency. He talked to three different people then sent Larry to wait in a small room. It wasn't long before a tall, dumb looking man came in.

"Are you Mayer?"

"I am."

"You are in a lot of trouble here!" he snapped.

"For what?"

"Entering an Embassy with a pistol."

"I was authorized to carry that pistol anywhere on US or foreign soil. I handed over the pistol as soon as I was requested to do so," Larry answered.

"I don't care what you were authorized to do, Mayer. I'm gonna' see you in prison!"

"You have no authority to arrest me, so lay off the macho jerk cop attitude!" Larry snapped.

"You want to say that again?"

"No, I want to break your stupid face," Larry said as he got into his face.

The man backed off a step then the door opened.

"Alright Armstrong, you won't be needed here," the Envoy said.

The man left without saying anything more.

"That asshole really has a problem," Larry remarked.

"He's just trying to do his job."

"No, he's another small minded asshole that gets a little bit of power and thinks he's God. I'll be sure to mention him in my report," Larry said but he knew that there probably wouldn't be any report by him.

"We have orders to ask you no questions. You can sleep in the office of the Charge de Affaires. The chairs recline and there is water and a bathroom. Somebody will be in between nine and ten this morning to talk to you."

"Alright," Larry said.

The secretary took him to office and he decided to sleep on the couch. He found a pack of peanut butter cookies and he ate all of them then he drank some water and lay down. At nine o'clock, the same secretary came in with coffee and a bagel. Larry ate the bagel and drank the coffee then the secretary left.

He had been sitting in the office for nearly a half hour when a navy commander and a woman came in with Shorty. Instinctively he stood up at attention.

"Mister Mayer, this is Margaret Kerscher from the AEC. You know Commander Thornton?"

"I don't think so," Larry said.

"You had better. He's here to identify you," Shorty said.

"He is Mayer," the commander said.

"You know me from where?" Larry asked.

"The LDH-4 Boxer."

"The Boxer was a new ship then. I came onboard in March and left in June. A lot of people were coming and going at that time."

"Tell me something I don't know," the commander requested.

"There were three women Helos. Shirley Stewart, Nancy Olds and Amy Bell."

"How the hell do you remember that?"

"Because I'm married to Shirley Stewart," Larry replied.

"Shock me, you son of a sea cook. I'm needing the poop here," he stated.

"A recovery operation for two Nukes, Mark 28 type. One of your fellows dropped them into two thousand feet of water off the coast of Sri Lanka. I went down in a hardsuit and hooked onto them."

"Who was in charge of this operation?"

"General Lester Barber and a 'three bar', Barry Holscomb. I didn't see or talk to anybody else. At least not on the vessel."

"What did they tell you?"

"It was a deliberate drop. The eggs were phonies. Nothing but trackers with Torpex filling. I blew the operation according to them."

"Was that Barber or Holscomb?" Thornton asked.

"Both of them in fact," Larry replied.

The Commander opened the folder and showed the pictures to Larry.

"Are those the bombs?" he asked.

Larry picked up the magnifying glass on the desk and looked at the bureau numbers on the tail.

"Yes, CN-8503 and CN-8505. Those are it," Larry stated.

"Those are real bombs, in fact," Thornton told him.

Larry froze a moment. He thought about the laws covering weapons of mass destruction.

"At that depth, the seawater would enter the shell and destroy the Deuterium Lithide and the fissionable material. All they would have is a very expensive shell," he said.

"We got two government agencies and three different stories. If that don't beat all," Larry remarked.

"Now you can deal with the AEC. Inspector Kerscher has her own reports to do," Shorty said.

"You can leave the binders," she said.

"Don't take any guff from this guy," Shorty said then they left.

"Please sit. We have a lot of things to go over. I'm just taking a statement now. Our guys in the field are still getting things sorted out, so it's still an on-going operation. When you leave here, say nothing about anything you have heard or the names of anybody that you have met."

"Affirmative, I know the drill."

She pulled a binder out of the stack.

"Commander Thornton said that you're a real corker. The kind of guy that would do an operation like this. I see that you have a baby that is seven months old and you have been married for fifteen months. You're a little old for this, I should think."

"The atmospheric suit allows diving at any rated depth without the problems..."

"I meant knocking up younger women. Do you think this is funny?" she asked.

"Mommy and daddy in law wanted grandchildren. Her former husband was adamant about having no children. Is this going in your report?"

"You would be surprised, Mister Mayer. Do you drink?"

"Hardly at all since I've been married. Very moderate before that, on the navy scale."

"Hardly at all?" she questioned, raising her eye brows.

"A beer once or twice a month and yes I do have firearms in my house."

"Some people mean 'hardly at all before six o'clock'," she replied.

"I am proned to giving straight answers to questions."

"I'm glad to hear that. According to the information I have here, it would take forty minutes to lower a Recovery Vehicle to two thousand feet. That seems to be a lot of time."

"It is equivalent to trying to control a puppet from a fifteen story window," Larry informed her.

"How long did it take to lower you?"

"About twenty minutes."

"And twenty minutes to raise you and bring you aboard?"

"That is correct, yes."

"So that means approximately two hundred and forty minutes in the suit?" she asked.

"Twenty more minutes for the checks topside and an hour to secure the bombs on deck. I saved a few minutes by riding up on the RRV."

"Why did you do that?"

"I could tell by the lights that it had stopped below the surface for ten minutes. When I rode it up, it stopped at a hundred feet and I encountered two men in scuba gear. I drove one off by ripping off his regulator. The other one stayed to fight, so I locked on to him and brought him up with the RRV. Barber and Holscomb told me later that he died."

"Is that all they told you?"

"At first they tried to deny, in front of all those other guys, that there was a diver. That was kinda' retarded, don't ya' think?"

"What was their explanation for that?"

"They are democrats. I was to not question any ridiculous lie they tell."

Margaret looked at him quizzically.

"They gave me that story about the bombs being Trackers. I didn't buy any of it, of course," Larry explained.

"Five hours seems like a long time to be in a suit and be at that depth," she remarked after a minute.

"Yeah, there's not too many fun-city aspects to those kinda' jobs."

"According to what the Charge de Affaires wrote, you claimed that you killed three Thai nationals last night at the Sugi Fora Hotel."

"Yes, I got a phone call before midnight. I was expecting a phone call, but nobody answered when I said 'hello'. I grabbed the Ruger pistol and pushed the door open slowly with my foot. The hall was completely dark, so I turned on the flashlight and saw these three young guys pulling butterfly knives. I shot all three of them then got the hell outta' there," Larry explained.

"The Bangkok police have confirmed that three young men were found dead in the second story hallway of the Sugi Fora hotel. Neither the clerk or anybody else saw anything or heard anything," Margaret informed him.

"Yeah, that figures. It could have been me lying dead in the hallway."

"Yes, one diver and three punk hoodlums are dead because of you. You have done a lot of killing in the past, I see," she said

"Sometimes it's a mission and sometimes it can't be helped."

"We'll have to keep you here until we get this sorted out."

"That will be fine. Just keep Barber, Holscomb, Putzer and the rest of them away from me."

"We can have your wife informed that you are safe and being held at this embassy, for the time being," Margaret suggested.

"Thanks, I'm sure that she would appreciate that."

"I think we're done here for now," she said as she closed the binder and stood up.

"One more thing."

"Yes."

"Can I have one of those diplomatic chits?" Larry asked.

"I'll have the Secretary get you one," she said then she took him back to Shorty.

When they got to the office of the Charge de Affaires, Smythe was writing down some numbers.

"My phone has been ringing nonstop. I have a call back for you," he said as he picked up the phone and hit the button. He handed the receiver to Larry.

"Security code," a woman's voice requested.

"I don't have any security code. You called me."

"Your extension?"

"I don't have any. I'm Larry Mayer. Somebody there called me."

"One moment."

"Hold for Mister Smith...What is it!" a man shouted.

"This is Larry Mayer. You called me."

"Mayer! What the fuck do you think you're doing. Who told you to go to the consulate?"

"I had just killed three guys in my hotel. They were coming after me. I sure in the hell wasn't gonna' hang around there."

"You should have contacted Barber!"

"My life was in danger. I had to get to a safe place immediately," Larry said.

Actually, since Barber had reserved him the hotel room, and the killers knew where to find him, Larry was having doubts about Barber.

"I'll send a car for you. It will take you to the airport. At the WorldJet counter, you will find a ticket to New Delhi then on to Rabat. Do you understand?"

"Yes, I do."

"Don't fuck this up, Mayer," he said then hung up.

"What a grouch. Let him shoot his way out of the shit and see how he feels," Larry said as he handed the phone back to Smythe.

"I already have orders to send you with the driver when he arrives."

"I don't know this guy. I don't know if I can trust him."

"You can always leave here on your own volition," Smythe said.

"This Smith claims that they have a ticket for Rabat. That's heading in the right direction," Larry reasoned.

In twenty minutes, a car came to the side entrance, which was used for important people. The guard went to the car with Larry and a porter carried his bags. The driver, a Thai, said nothing when Larry got in and on the way to the airport. At the airport, he told Larry that he would get his bags. He carried Larry's bags to the counter and refused a tip then he left. The woman at the WorldJet counter was an American and she got the ticket for Larry with no problem. His bags were run through the X-ray and he went through the metal detectors and into the gate area. He found his gate and waited for the announcement, in five languages, that his flight was ready to board. Instead, there was an announcement that the flight to New Delhi was oversold and ten people would have to wait for another flight. Larry certainly expected to see his name on the board, but it wasn't on there. He watched as crying old women and children were escorted from the gate area. A half hour later they got on the plane. The passengers were mostly old women who could barely walk or hear and young women with babies that cried incessantly. Welcome to the friendly skies, Larry thought when the wheels finally got off the ground. The old man next to him had some problem with the G forces and seemed to panicking.

"Don't worry. If the engines quit, they'll let you get out and walk," Larry quipped.

The old guy looked at him then decided to keep his apprehension to himself. At cruising altitude, the Indians got up and seemed to be all over the place. The flight attendant invited him into first class for a drink. He accepted just to get out of their way. They had fold down tables in the rear of first class where they served the drinks. A British fellow invited him to sit down.

"I'm Allen Horton," he said, offering his hand.

"Larry Mayer," Larry said as they shook hands.

"I knew you were an American. Only an American would ride anything else but first class on these flights."

"Yes, I'll have to talk to my girl about that," Larry quipped.

"What sort of business are you in?"

"Deep sea diving," Larry replied.

"Oil rigs. Those kind of things."

"Yes, oil rigs have been a large part of our business. We did some diving for these television programs. Filming the bottom at a thousand and two thousand feet. That was east of Sri Lanka."

"That sounds terribly interesting," Allen said.

"Not really. There isn't much to see at that depth. Just a bloody pain actually."

"I heard that there is still fighting on Sri Lanka."

"Yes, we flew across the place. You couldn't drive across it. Too dangerous," Larry said.

"I lived and worked in South Africa for years. It used to be a great place. The news media always talked about that terrible place with Apartheid. People were happy and working. It was a safe place then. Now four or five hundred people are murdered every week. It has become just like the rest of Africa and it was because of Nelson Mandela. That bastard let it happen because he wouldn't crack down on the blacks to keep them in line."

"Well, Africa is the most mineral rich continent in the world," Larry said.

"A lot of bloody good that has been doing them. Do you know that Africa is the only continent where the population is decreasing?"

"Because of war and famine?"

"Partly, but mostly because of AIDS," he said.

"Africa is showing us the way," Larry quipped.

"I suppose it would be amusing, unless you're trying to do business there."

"I'm headed to Morocco myself then on to home."

"Where's home?" he asked.

"Nantucket Island."

"That was a whaling port?"

"Before the Civil War. It is mostly a retreat for the wealthy now," Larry replied.

At the next table, a black guy wearing African garb began laughing loudly. He was punched by a woman with a headdress. She got up and left.

"That is my wife," he said in a thick accent.

"She looks like she's waiting for you with a stick," Larry said.

"Don't worry, that is her way," he assured them.

Horton looked at him like he was contemptible vermin that needed smashed immediately.

"You are also headed to Africa?" Larry asked.

"Yes, we are headed back to Liberia. I am Innocent George."

"I am Larry Mayer."

"What sort of work do you do?" Innocent asked.

"I am a deep sea diver."

"Why would you do dangerous work like that?"

"Because the truth is down there," Larry replied

"How is the truth in the ocean?"

"When a vessel sinks or something is lost overboard, it is preserved in the sea. Man will always try to alter things to fit his immediate purpose, but in the sea, the truth remains preserved where men cannot touch it."

The woman came back and hit Innocent in the side of the head with a clutch purse.

"I am coming...Excuse me, gentlemen," he said as he got up then he went with her.

"I thought the Flight Attendant was going to get them," Larry said.

"People like that are exactly what is wrong with Africa."

"What's the plan? We wait for the Africans to kill themselves off then we move in and bring back the big game and mine the wealth?"

"There won't be anything left to save," Horton opined.

"Yeah, but our government has got to stay out of Africa. We got burned in Somalia and it can't get any better."

"I got some business friends to meet in New Delhi, if you're not in a hurry to get to Morocco."

"The plane leaves an hour and a half after this one gets there. I hope they get the luggage transferred. These blighters have been known to take a break or get lost and leave the luggage on the trailer," Larry said.

Larry had experienced New Delhi before. Outside of the airport, the city reeked of feces, garbage and death. All cities in India were like that. Thousands of people died in the streets and contributed to the smell and the disease. Having experienced it once, he avoided it now. When he met Mother Theresa in California, he knelt before the little woman out of admiration, he recalled.

When the pilot announced that they were approaching New Delhi, Larry went back to his seat in business class. If anything, the old people were slower and more confused, the babies were fussing louder and two dogs were barking continually. The only thing missing were the chickens and goats, Larry thought. Fortunately, upon landing, the flight attendants held some of the more burdensome people in their seats and Larry was able to deplane in a few minutes. He went to the designated gate and took a seat, but a flight attendant immediately came up to him and told him that someone wanted to speak to him on the phone. He looked around for the courtesy phone, but she indicated the counter phone. Larry picked up the phone.

"Hello."

"Hold for the supervisor....Mayer, this is Smith. Did you have any problems?"

"I didn't have to sit on the roof, if that's what you mean."

"Good! Listen, don't talk to anybody. Don't tell anybody your name. No bik the language, got it?"

"Yes, Great One. I understand," Larry quipped.

"Wait at the gate in Rabat. Someone will be there eventually."

"Check."

"Stay out of trouble."

"Will do."

Click

"Good-bye," Larry said into a dead phone.

He put down he receiver.

"If you are hungry, the crews lounge is the only place to eat," she said.

"You are an American?"

"Yes, my ten hours will be up and I'm getting on the plane with you. Only four more hours and I'm off. I'll get you a pass for the crew's lounge," she said.

She went over to what looked like a library card catalog and pulled out a pass.

"Just tell them that Indian food makes you sick."

"I'm sure it would. Thank you," Larry said.

"It's down that way. You got forty five minutes," she said.

"Catch you later," Larry said, smiling.

As he walked down the concourse, he wondered if the Flight Attendant was being nice because he got a call on the airline phone. When he got to the Crew's lounge, only about half of the table and counter stools were occupied. There were cockpit and cabin crews of different nationalities and wearing a variety of uniforms. He was the only one in Service Khaki and several people looked at him because of it, he thought. He got some pizza and root beer and sat at a table by himself, but close to aircrew that looked American.

"You're American, sit over here," a pilot said. He was about five feet eight and slender build as the police say.

Larry picked up his plate and joined them.

"Nobody but an American would wear Service Khaki in this place."

"I seem to be recognizable wherever I go," Larry said as he sat down at their table.

"Sure, you're an old school Navy guy for sure. You probably retired more than ten years ago. You're in good shape for your age, so you probably engage in some activity like parachuting."

"Scuba diving. I see no reason to leave a perfectly good airplane in order to land with a set of drapes," Larry stated.

"Buzz Larkin," he said as he extended his hand over the table.

"Larry Mayer," Larry said as they shook hands.

"This is Flo Evers and Susan McDonald."

"Hello," Larry said, smiling at them.

He had a feeling in his ear like a flea kicking around in there. Something was familiar or sounded familiar here, but it wasn't coming together yet.

"Where did you come from?" Buzz asked.

"Bangkok."

"We call that the 'monkey run'. All kinds of unusual characters on those flights."

"There certainly was on this one," Larry stated.

"Where do you live?"

"Nantucket."

"We're west coasters, except for Susan here. She's from Virginia."

Something like a shock hit Larry. The others looked at him. He recognized the name and this woman matched the description that Brown had given him. Of course, she had nothing to do with Joe's demise, but he couldn't help himself.

"Don't I know you?" Larry asked

"Men say that all the time. You'll have to do better than that," Susan said.

"No, you wouldn't know me, probably, but you might remember some friends of mine, Joe Cole and Luis Valero. You flew from Florida to Virginia with them in a Piper Arrow a couple years ago."

"Yes, I did. Eight months later, I was told that they went down in the ocean."

"Yes, they did. Joe was an old navy buddy of mine. I found their airplane on the bottom and a navy recovery ship brought it up. I was told your name and showed a picture, but I didn't recognize you at the time, of course. It is nice meeting you," Larry said.

"There's only seven billion people in the world, so what a coincidence," Flo remarked.

"I can't believe all the times I have run into people that I knew or had some unusual connection with, at an airport," Larry said.

"Well this one must be right up there," Susan said.

"Yes, there must be a God," Larry quipped.

"I'll bet you fly," Buzz said.

"For the last thirty years. Just doing my annual PPL checkout rides most of the time."

"Any bigger stuff?"

"Yes, I got my twin certification. My wife has a Beechcraft Baron and I did some check-out flights in a Piper Seminole belonging to Melissa Macklin of Alexander Bay, New York," Larry explained.

"Who is your wife?"

"Shirley Douglas. She was a Helo in the navy. We've been married a year and a half.

"A Baron is a big chunk of change. A Seminole costs half of what a Baron costs."

"Shirley takes care of it. Keeps it hangared. Melissa has her own airfield and hangar. She owns the Schooner Bay Hotel and part of a casino in Canada."

"Shirley must have some assets."

"I couldn't tell ya'. I never asked her before we were married. We didn't have a Pre-nup or anything like that. She handles the money," Larry said.

"Where are you headed?" Buzz asked.

"Morocco, Rabat."

"We're going to Cairo. Catch you on the flip side," Buzz said.

"I'm sure we'll be meeting again," Larry said.

After Buzz and the women left, Larry finished his pizza and went back to the gate. The flight attendant smiled and greeted him at the counter.

"The food was great," Larry said.

"It's the only place to eat in this airport."

"I'll tell all my friends," Larry said, smiling.

At boarding time, she let Larry board first with the 'special' passengers. Once again, there were few white people in business class, but the passengers seemed more normal, for lack of a better word, to Larry.

Many Moroccans dress in western clothes, although some women were in traditional Burkhas and the men in Thawbs. Everybody seemed tired and wanting to rest. Larry knew it was going to be a long flight, so he reclined the seat as much as he could and took a nap. By the time they had crossed the Indian Ocean and were more than halfway across North Africa, the flight Attendant was off of work and sat next to Larry.

Hello again."

"Did they cut you loose?"

"Yes, I'm slumming for the next twenty four hours. I'm Heather by the way."

"Larry."

"You look like a man on his way home."

"That's what my masters tell me. Not that I can trust them one bit. Kind of like your job, except that they can and do change their minds at any time. I could be going back to the far east."

"What do you do?"

"I'm a diver."

"Your employers may want you to dive again?"

"Probably not. There were local government problems. Those type of people don't want us around when they show up," Larry explained.

"The guy on the phone didn't sound too happy," she observed.

"Yes, people get unhappy when things don't go as planned."

"I get that all the time."

"Back in Bangkok, they had to pull ten passengers off of the plane. I was surprised that I didn't get bumped since it was a last minute booking," Larry said.

"You were 'red card'. You would never get bumped unless it was for a really important person."

"I'll have to ask for that the next time I fly," Larry said.

By the time they landed in Rabat, it was 0650. As they came down the ramp, they were greeted by the sun rising over the desert. Larry retrieved his luggage and waited at the check-in area for someone to show up. After an hour, he picked up his bags and decided that he would find some place more comfortable to stay. Going outside, he saw a car pull up in the drop-off lane and a man got out. He looked to be in a hurry. Larry couldn't believe his eyes.

"Harry, the airport ain't going anywhere," Larry said.

Harry stopped and looked at him.

"McLeod is missing."

"Where was he at?" Larry asked.

"Meknes."

"How long does it take to get there?"

"An hour," Brown answered.

"Let's go," Larry said.

The Moroccans had constructed a decent road to Meknes, but the eighty miles took somewhat more than an hour in the 'company' car. When they got there, the town looked quiet. Brown went to the shop of a leather worker and asked for a man by name. A young fellow spoke to Brown then he drove the car for them. They went to an airfield that was five miles away and saw a helicopter and an old Piper Twin Cherokee sitting in front of a hangar. Brown surveyed the scene with binoculars. Some men appeared to be milling around the helicopter and a couple men walked toward their car. Brown pulled out an S&W model 19.

"Do you know how to fly that airplane?"

"Yes," Larry replied.

Brown pointed the pistol and fired, but he missed. The two men ran back toward the helicopter.

"They got McLeod. Take this and cover me," Brown said.

"What do you think you're gonna' do?"

"I'll see if I can get to the helicopter."

Unfortunately, at least four men got into the helicopter and it took off before Brown got anywhere near it. Larry took the pistol and started running toward the airplane. Two men were trying to run to the airplane from the opposite direction, so Larry raised the pistol and fired a shot at them. He missed, but the next time he would be much closer, so the two fellows turned and ran. The airplane was a twin Cherokee, which was the predecessor of the Seminole. Larry wasn't sure if it was airworthy, or if he could fly it. This was no time to have to read the manual, he thought as he looked into the door on the right side to see if anyone was I there. He ran around the outside to see if everything was still attached and he ran into Brown.

"Let's go!" Brown ordered.

"Uh...Who's aircraft is this?"

"Don't know, don't care. Start it up and let's go," he insisted.

"Alright, keep a lookout for those two guys coming back," Larry said as he stepped up onto the wing.

He ducked and moved to the pilot's seat. The cockpit seemed even smaller than the Seminole's. He looked in the pouch and found the usual documents and the checklist, in Arabic.

"Great, it's in Arabic!" he exclaimed.

"This is no time for reading the damn manual!"

"This is an older plane than I have flown. I'll need a minute," Larry said.

On these older Pipers, most of switches were on the left, below the pilot's window. Larry turned on the master switch, magnetos, alternators and the navigation lights. Below the instrument cluster were two of the manual primer plungers. He pushed in the left one three times then set the throttles at half an inch forward and pushed the props and mixture levers all the way forward. He pressed the left engine start switch. The propeller turned twice and the engine started up. He checked the instruments and the vacuum reading to make sure that everything was working.

"What's the hold-up," Brown snapped.

"This isn't a fucking lawnmower," Larry said, adding-"I hope you got an idea where they're going."

"North," Brown said.

"That narrows it down to half a million square miles," Larry remarked.

He hit the right primer three times and the starter switch for the right engine and it started up just as readily as the left engine. He checked the fuel selectors and the trim wheels between the seats. He did a quick check of flaps and control surfaces and checked the fuel. Fortunately the tanks were full.

"That Eurocopter probably won't be going any more than 100 knots. Assuming that he's heading for Tangiers or some other place on the coast, we can probably catch him," Larry said as he started taxiing. When he was on the runway, he gunned it and assuming no wind or obstacles or god knows what else, accelerated down the runway, heading north.

CHAPTER EIGHT

"There's a helicopter, a ways off to the left," Brown said while looking in the binoculars.

Larry saw that it was at nearly the same altitude, so he turned toward it.

"How do you know it's them."

"It's an old police trick to come up behind or beside somebody. Crooks always have an inclination to do something stupid," Larry said.

"What the hell are you going to do? We stole this airplane, so we aren't calling the cops."

"Push and enterprise. That from Mark Twain: River boat pilot," Larry said.

"That's just great!"

"Don't worry. If we get away with this, it will be our little secret. Nothing about it on the report."

They were flying almost perpendicular to the helicopter now and it suddenly turned to the left and the pilot poured on the coal. Larry could see that it was a Eurocopter AS350.

"There's an old Air Force Base about ten miles from here. If you can force him down, that would be the place to do it," Brown said.

"Do you suppose this fellow is a stunt flyer?" Larry asked.

"Straight and level is about all you can expect."

"Do you know what colliding with another vessel is called?" Larry asked.

"I can't say that I do."

"Dumb seamanship. I'm going for his tail rotor."

"You trying to shoot it off?"

"Ram it," Larry replied.

"Er-uh, is there another way?"

"Yeah, but the survivability sucks."

"We don't even know if McLeod is in there or if he's alive." Brown said.

"We'll make them tell us...Ty is the only person on this planet that I owe a favor. We have to get him back," Larry said as the helicopter and the tail rotor, in particular, were looking awful big to them.

In a couple seconds, the nose of the airplane was struck by the tail rotor, perhaps ten times, denting and gashing into the aluminum skin and the fiberglass structure. The airplane shook, but it stayed on course as Larry backed off on the throttle a little. The tail of the helicopter swayed left and right, menacingly.

"He heard you knocking that time," Brown said.

"He's slowing down. The bent tail rotor is causing him some control problems, I think," Larry said, adding-"How good are you with that Model nineteen?"

"How good do I have to be?" Brown asked.

"Real good," Larry said.

They came up on the right side of the helicopter and it appeared that one of the Arabs was trying to push McLeod out of the door. Larry set the autopilot and aimed the pistol through the Emergency Access Opening in the window. Fortunately, the bastard made the mistake of exposing his body for a moment and Larry fired. The terrorist clutched at his chest then fell on the floor of the helicopter. The AS350 veered away and Larry decided to give it some room since they were coming to the airfield.

The helicopter slowed considerably and Larry cut the throttle and side-slipped the Piper to lose the altitude and speed quickly. He figured to come to a stop near the hangars, where the chopper would probably land. This pilot lacked imagination, so Larry figured that he wouldn't do anything clever like land on a building.

"He shot the guy who was trying to throw you out. He brought down the helicopter and he killed the two guys back there," Brown said.

"What have you done for me lately, Nigga'?" McLeod asked.

"I'm taking you to Tangiers. The sun and fun place for white women. You can really practice the chokeholds there, Marine," Larry replied.

"I don't know. I've been put through the wringer and I still can't figure out what's going on here."

"It's simple, Ty. Who's the president?" Larry asked rhetorically.

"Just like 9/11, I suppose."

"Yeah, blame it all on Bush, like he was the only one who had his head up his ass. The Air Egypt thing and the eight guys in Seattle. Congress wouldn't even think about doing anything about it because all congress could think about was fucking with Bush," Larry replied.

"I suppose you're right about that, Chief."

"Of course, I'm right. Do you see Obama here? Do you think it was him that sent me?"

"Let's save the political discussion for later, guys," Brown suggested.

"We have the altitude to get over those hills now," Larry said, adding- "The real estate doesn't look too good from up here."

"Somebody could be down there with an SA-8 or a Stinger Missile," Brown said.

"I have no idea what the heat signature is. Certainly much less than a warplane, but that wasn't a design criteria for an aircraft like this," Larry said.

They came to the coast, just east of the point, so Larry turned left and got a visual on Tangiers with no trouble. Brown directed him to the airfield and Larry radioed to the control tower and gave them the 'magic' registration number and they were cleared to land. The hangar doors were open and

Larry taxied the Twin Cherokee right into the hangar and shutdown the engines.

"Who's the contact dude here?" Larry asked.

"I know him. I'll handle it. Who's your contact?" Brown asked.

"General Anthony Barber. He's a former Air Force dude. Not your department. I don't know who he's working for now," Larry replied.

"I'll have our Chief contact his chief. When I'm here, I have to go through the proper Channels," Brown said as he opened the rear door.

"It's so much easier working in the field. I gotta' call the little woman and see what's for supper. How about you, Ty?" Larry asked as McLeod got out the rightside door.

"I'm divorced."

"Oh, that's too bad. You could tell the family that you were saved by superhero, Larry Mayer," Larry said as he stooped down and exited after him.

They had to wait by the aircraft until somebody of sufficient authority came out to clear them. The regular personnel walked by, looking indifferent to them. It took five minutes for two men in suits to show up.

"Marv and Kevin, this is Larry Mayer of Nantucket."

"I have heard of you," Marv said as they shook hands.

"I can't say I've heard of you," Larry wisecracked.

"I have run into you, but you probably don't remember," Kevin said as they shook hands.

"What was I doing at the time?" Larry asked.

"You had some Cubans against a wall and you kicking them in the ass," he replied.

"Oh yes, I was having trouble getting their attention. They became much better listeners after that," Larry said.

"Haven't you heard of the Geneva Convention 1949?"

"Of course, I was requiring them to be silent. They were some elite Castro's guard. I required them to behave as a defeated enemy and do what they were told. Reagan was happy, so others should be," Larry said.

"Are we cleared here?' Brown asked.

"Sure, let's go to the officers club. You can tell us all about it," Marvin said as they started walking toward the hangar door. As soon as they were clear, the hangar personnel seemed to descend on the Twin Cherokee. Larry wondered how soon it would be before somebody noticed the ding in the nose.

The Officers Club was another small hangar that was used as a mess hall and a recreation area. Larry and Tyrone had supper in there while Harry went with Marv and Keith. Larry hoped that Harry would be the one writing the reports. He signed on to dive, not write fricking reports.

"You seem quieter than usual," Larry observed.

"I have to go home and take care of some things. My ex wants more child support."

"That must be tough. I never had problems like that, thank goodness."

"I know you can tell me what's wrong with me," McLeod said.

"There's not much wrong with you, except that you believe in that jerk in the White House and those Jag offs from Pittsburgh. I was eleven years old when I stopped believing in an ideal world. Utopia isn't just an election away in any fucking system. Deal with it and keep going in the right direction."

"Women have me stumped at the moment."

"When I was a kid, my father set me on a horse and said-'Keep your legs on both sides and your mind in the middle'. When I as older, he said-'You have to get into a woman's head before you can get into her pants.' It sounds overly simple, but that's the way it's gotta' be done," Larry said.

"You don't seem to have respect for authority," McLeod opined.

"Have you ever heard of the Milgram experiment?"

"I can't say that I have."

"Volunteers, who were called testers, were to teach the subjects various things. The supervisors authorized the testers to use electric shocks to motivate the subjects to learn faster. It was based on the experiments the Nazis had done. The result was that seventy percent of the testers used electric shocks even though they could hear the subjects screaming when they did. Of course, the subjects and supervisors were fake, but the testers didn't know that. They responded that way because they were pressured to get results. Power corrupts and absolute power really pisses me off," Larry explained.

"And the way these people treat you, pisses you off?"

"Anybody who thinks that they own my ass, pisses me off. They're operating outside of the law and they can't even practice common decency," Larry said.

After supper, Larry went to the administrator's desk and asked to see the man in charge. Everybody looked at him strangely, but eventually Keith came out.

"Yes, Larry. What can I do for you?"

"I would like to call my wife."

"I would like to help you, but there are a couple problems with that. You see, this is an overseas operational area. People here are usually away from their families for a year or eighteen months and only communicate by mail. Also, non-essential communications are being held with the Secretary of State visiting the area." he explained.

"Let's cut the crap. This isn't 1960. I know better than that, Keith. Hillary is in India. Not even the same fucking continent," Larry snapped.

"Yes, well, before you landed there was a bulletin to all agencies that you were missing from the airport in Rabat. Some people are very upset about this. We have orders to keep you here until your people show up and retrieve you."

"I suppose that this confinement also means no communications?" Larry asked.

"It's standard procedure."

"Thank you for your honesty. Just be straight with me, Keith. I have heard it all by now," Larry said.

"Certainly, is there anything else you need?"

"Accommodations, and I left my bags back at Meknes, so I have no clothes except what I'm wearing."

"We'll get you a room. You won't have to sleep in the barracks. I'll see if we can get you some service khakis. I'll get you a voucher for razors, deodorant, anything you need at the PX."

"Thank you. I'm much obliged," Larry said.

"Not at all," Keith said.

After he left, the guy at the desk gave Larry a voucher for the PX and told him the room number and building number. When Larry got to the room, the bed was already made. He set the bag of PC items on the steel desk and checked the bed for bugs. Typical government room, he thought then he went back to the 'Officers Club'. After getting a bottle of Reisling, he sat at a table. No one seemed to notice him and he thought about home and his family. He was about ready to leave when Brown and another man came to his table, so he stood up.

"Larry, this is Barry."

"Larry, Barry and Harry. It sounds like Sesame Street," Larry quipped as they shook hands.

"It's Bartholomew, but I've always been called Barry."

"Sit down if you're staying," Larry said and they sat down.

"What's the good news?"

"You," Barry said.

"I'm just a poor wayfaring stranger....Have you got my walking papers?"

"Your people will come get you as soon as they can," Barry replied.

"I'm not too fond of their way of doing things."

"According to Harry, you're a real ball of fire. He gives you all the credit for saving McLeod."

"That's life! Ya' gotta' love at least one Marine. Where is Ty?"

"Flying back to Washington."

"What, he gets to go, and I'm stuck here in this wasteland! Think of all the fun we could be having."

"You don't frequent those places," Harry said.

"Yeah, but it fools them. My granddaughter says if you're old, bald and ugly, you're outta' here. Nobody wants you. Kids are taught that intelligence and ability don't count for anything."

"We know better," Barry said.

"Yeah, we always knew better, but we always had to kill those who didn't," Larry lamented.

"You sound like you need some sleep. You're getting a little punchy," Harry said.

"Yeah, I'm not as young as I used to be. Let me know if the place is burning down," Larry quipped.

"Sure thing, Chief."

Larry went to his room and flopped down on the bed. God, he wished he could call Shirley. He wanted to hear her voice again. He looked at the desk and saw a phone. That wasn't there before, he knew. He got up and picked up the receiver-nothing. The damn CIA shit doesn't work, he swore. He laid on the bed again. I can't take the booze anymore, he thought. I'm more lit than I was at my bachelor party. He remembered beating all of his friends at arm wrestling. They had some real corkers in the navy. In San Diego, a bunch of chiefs, most of them instructors, were leaving for assignments in numbered fleets. The party went on for three days. Once one of those things got started, it took an act of God to stop it.

Around midnight the phone rang. Larry thought he was hearing things, so he tried to ignore it. A few minutes later, it rang again.

"Hello."

"This is Smith. What the fuck are you doing?"

"At the moment, sleeping," Larry answered.

"I made it very clear to wait at the airport. Do you have trouble understanding instructions!"

"I ran into a friend from the CIA. These terrorists were trying to throw him out of a helicopter. Time was of the essence," Larry replied.

"The CIA takes care of their operatives and I'm responsible for you. Got it, Jack!"

"Oh contrare. Team work is required. You gotta' give the other man a hand sometimes and go fuck yourself, asshole!" Larry snapped.

Smith hung up the phone.

Larry wondered if the phone was working now, so he tried to dial his home phone.

"We're sorry, the number you dialed is not available. Please hang up and check your directory." Larry thought about who this Smith was. He must be pissed off now. Larry knew that it wasn't much, but he jammed the chair under the door knob and he went back to sleep.

At five thirty he was woke up by the sound of people passing by his door. It must be the morning shift getting up, he thought. He put on his unwashed service khakis and brushed his teeth. He went back to the Officers Club and had a breakfast of scrambled eggs and Canadian bacon. When he was done, he looked at the clock. It was 0600 and he saw General Barber and another man, who was wearing Ray Bans, coming his way.

"Well General, you certainly get around," Larry said.

"So do you, in fact."

"Just a little favor for a friend. That Smith didn't sound too happy. I guess he doesn't have any friends."

"We have a plane outside. This is Frank Elliot. He'll be flying it. We have to leave real soon here."

"I have some personal care items in my room. I got separated from my bags in Meknes. All my clothes, watch, shoes..."

"We can get those things when we land. We have to leave as soon as possible."

"Wait a minute, I been run around here enough. I better get an explanation or I'm not going anywhere," Larry insisted.

"I can't go into it right now, but suffice it to say that we're on our way home," Barber said.

"Alright, but I'll need to use the head," Larry said.

After he was done, they walked out to the hangar.

"I never thought that my stomach would miss cornbread and clam chowder," Larry said.

Barber just looked at him.

"You know you can't get it anywhere else but the east coast. What a pathetic world this is."

"When we get back, I'll make sure that you get a lifetime supply," Barber said.

"I take it that you heard about Brown and me rescuing McLeod. Now that was a real old time operation. Birds of prey! Wit and nerve pitted against the forces of evil. I should get the fucking Congressional Medal of Honor. I can't get crap because I'm no longer in the service. Doesn't that suck shit?" Larry asked rhetorically.

"It certainly does," Barber said.

"Same difference. I'm not doing it for the money, so give me the chest cabbage," Larry suggested.

"I'm sure that the CIA will give you the world on a silver platter."

"They'll give me a ping pong ball on a paper plate. That's a Cessna 210."

"Good observation."

"Where we going, Elliot?"

"Agadir, on the coast," Barber answered for him.

"That's a touristy place. I wanted something representative of the people and their culture," Larry quipped.

"I see that your sense of humor hasn't been affected," Barber said as he opened the door.

"That comes from being around all you humorless people. Oh, I get the front," Larry said as he got in after Barber.

Frank did the walk around then got in the pilot's seat.

"We'll refuel when we get to Agadir," Frank said.

"Check," Barber replied.

"How long you been flying, Frank?" Larry asked.

"Twenty years."

"I figured. You looked about forty"

Frank wasn't a very talkative type, he thought.

"Were you an instructor?" Larry asked.

Frank looked at him.

"No, I wasn't."

He started up the engine and taxied to the end of the runway. He did the usual run up and checks of the engine and control surfaces.

"You should have seen it, Barbie. I rammed the nose of that old twin Cherokee into the tail rotor of that Eurocopter. That caused them some control problems, I'll tell ya'."

Elliot put on the headphones and requested takeoff clearance. He was given clearance immediately. He gunned the throttle and the Cessna surged ahead. That early in the morning, it was still cool and the propeller grabbed for air as the plane accelerated down the runway. It lifted off with no stick and Elliot retracted the landing gear and got it into cruise climb immediately.

"It's like southern California in the old days. Me and Joe Cole used to fly those old NE-1's all over the place. We probably would have got there faster by car. Those crates cruised at eighty knots."

"Confirm our arrival at Agadir," Barber said.

"Check," Frank replied.

"What's your hurry? We gotta' do approach confirmation anyway. Can't those idiots read a flight plan?" Larry asked.

"We have to refuel. We want to be sure that we get a place in line. You have to be sure in these foreign places," Barber answered.

"Oh yeah, I suppose you do," Larry said.

"Where you from, Frank?" Larry asked.

"California."

"Wherebouts?"

"Fontana."

"No kiddin'. I knew this Japanese guy from there. His name was fukahora. Honest to god. Anyway, he had this old T-10 parachute, so I took it out on the lawn and folded it panel by panel like they taught us then I secured the shroud lines in the back flap and closed it. I told him that it hadn't been inspected, so don't let nobody jump it. Well these guys come in from a jump and one of them sees this chute and takes it out and jumps with it. Totally crazy! Do you know any of the guys in the parachute club?"

"I grew up there. I haven't been back there in twenty years," he replied.

"Frank is level three," Barber said.

"I was level five. I didn't have a crypto classification though. Hey, should I tell Shirley about ramming that twin Cherokee into the tail rotor? Do you think she would let me fly that Beechcraft again?" Larry quipped.

"I think that you should keep quiet about the entire operation for some time here," Barber replied.

"I used to tell Darla what I had done. Nobody cares to repeat war stories these days."

Frank had been busy texting someone on his cellphone.

"It looks like at least an hour and a half in Agadir," he said.

"Alright, we'll get off as soon as we can. You can read a book, Larry," Barber said as he handed him a woman's novel with a rather aroused young man and woman on the cover.

"I remember when I used to do that. I better not. Shirley will think that another woman has been teaching me something. I'll read the POH," Larry said as he picked up the pilot's handbook.

Agadir was a town which had been rebuilt as a vacation place for Germans after an earthquake had destroyed it in 1956. Larry was the only one that spoke German, so he helped get the airplane serviced and he found a good place to eat. People seemed to be friendly enough and he was shown many of the attractions there. No matter how much they made it sound like Germany, it was still a dusty desert town on the coast. People certainly seemed to enjoy the ocean and sunbathing and the casinos though. He ran into Barber in the restroom and Barber told him that they were ready to go. Larry mentioned that Frank seemed to be hiding something or was uneasy about something. Barber said that Frank was always like that and not to worry about it.

When they came back to the airfield, Frank was already at the Cessna and he seemed more restive than before. Barber stayed on the left side of the airplane and talked to him for a minute. Larry figured that he was seeing if Frank was up to flying after what he had said. He opened the right side door and was about to get in the back when Barber told him that he would take the back seat again. Frank got the engine started, but this time they had to wait for a commercial airliner which was coming in. After a ten minute delay, they were cleared to take-off and Frank got it into the air with no problem. The clean sea and sand look of the coast was apparent as they flew over it on a course of 255. Larry hadn't asked, but he knew that the only thing out there was the Canary Islands.

After about thirty minutes in the air, Larry saw two small islands in front of them and a larger island off to the left.

"Land Ho!" Larry quipped.

"We have a little ways to go. The small islands are uninhabited," Barber said.

They were at five thousand feet and about six miles away from the islands when the engine suddenly quit.

"Can you get it started, Frank!?" Barber asked, excitedly.

"I don't know?" Elliot said as he tried to figure out why it had stopped.

Frank was doing a good job of holding it straight and level and milking all the distance he could get out of it.

"Can you make the beach? We gotta' make the beach. I don't want to go down in the ocean!" Barber implored him.

"We might... We might make it," Frank said.

"Larry, do something!" Barber implored.

"Feather the prop," Larry suggested.

"I'll never get it started if I do," Frank said.

"It ain't gonna' start. The wind milling is slowing us too much. Eating up our forward speed," Larry said.

"That island in front of us is our only hope," Frank said.

Larry saw the water bottle in the door pouch. It was only a third full, but he stuck it in his shirt. The lower they got, the faster the plane was dropping. Larry opened the door and held it ajar with his right hand and foot. The wheels were up, so the Cessna settled down easily as it hit the water. The water was pressing on the door as Larry forced it open with both hands and feet. The water really started pouring in then. He took a deep breath and jumped away from the airplane as far as he could. A wave broke over him and the airplane because they had come down in the surf line. He was held under for a minute by the turbulence but came up and got his breath again. He began swimming toward the shore and was hit by another breaker which sent him tumbling end over end. It took another minute but he came up to the surface again. He began swimming with all his strength, and had gotten only about sixty feet when another breaker hit him. This one, fortunately, was much smaller and he managed to get through it and keep swimming as fast as he could.

CHAPTER NINE

Larry made it to the shore and crawled a few more feet to be clear of the water. He rolled over and looked at the sea. He looked for any sign of the airplane or Turnbull and Elliot. He knew that at his age, he was just as susceptible to the shock and panic as any untrained person. He stood up shakily.

"Stand to, sailor. You've made it. You're alive and in one piece. You're gonna' get through this. It won't seem bad at all when you're telling the story to Shirley and the gang on Nantucket," he said out loud.

The sun seemed very hot, so he went to look for shade. He found a small palm of some sort and tore off some fronds and laid them on the sand so that he could sit down in its' shade. Drinking the water in the bottle, Larry laid down and closed his eyes. He wasn't sleeping very long when he was awakened by sand hitting him. He woke up and looked into the sun. He put his hand up to shield his eyes, but he still had difficulty seeing the man standing in the sun.

"Larry, me boy, you're a sad sight, you are."

He was trying to remember from whence he knew this Scottish guy.

"How did you get here? By boat?"

"Aye laddy, ya' haven't changed a bit, I'm seeing."

"I could use some water."

"Aye, it's water you're wanting now. There's a few wee matters we need to be discussing first. For instance, what happened to Turnbull and Elliot?"

"They were lost out there on the reef."

"Is that so? And how's that, Brolly?"

"When I got through the breakers, I turned and looked for them but I didn't see them. I had to get to shore myself before I lost what little strength I had left."

"A bonny tale to be sure, laddy. You swam away while they frantically called out for help, no doubt."

"I neither saw or heard them. The plane was sinking. I had to get away from it."

"Feckless, me boy. Nine men dead because of you."

"I was correct in everything I did and I have told the truth."

"Aye, ya' have, laddy. We all take oaths to tell the truth, to be sure, but that's not the party line, is it? Global warming and politically correct are what we want because there is no lie and there is no truth."

"The last guy that tried to convince me of that, lost his job and ended up picking up aluminum cans for a living."

"That's the sad state of affairs. Soon the economy will collapse, boy-oh. You'll be wishing that you were back out there in the breakers..."

Larry fell over and lay still for a long time. When he came to, he was very thirsty and it was dark. He went through his pockets and found his lighter, the mini-lite on his keys, his pocket knife, wallet, handkerchief, Passport, Chit and a pack of Juicy fruit. The sugar would be good if he had some water to go with it, he thought. He took his mini-lite and picked up his empty bottle and walked along the beach, but he found nothing and returned to where he had been. It wasn't long before a mist moved in from the sea. He found a plant with big oval leaves that were collecting the mist in small droplets. He partly folded the leaves lengthwise to form a trough and shook them gently so that the droplets came together and ran down the trough and into his water bottle. After an hour, he had a little more than an inch of water in the bottle. Just a couple fluid ounces. He thought about how to purify the water then he figured that it hadn't been on the ground, so he just drank it. Another hour yielded the same amount of water, so he capped the bottle and saved that. He returned where he had been and sat down on the palm fronds. The mist had ceased so he thought about survival and looked up at the sky. He could see the moon for a minute or less at a time before a cloud covered it again. He had never heard of large predators on these little islands off of Africa, but there could be poisonous snakes, scorpions and god knows what else, he thought. He found some dried driftwood and shaved off some match sized pieces to start burning. When he had got enough wood together, he lit the shavings with his lighter and put on some of the twigs and fanned it with a piece of bark. He had to fan for a while but he eventually got a self-sustaining fire going. Taking stock of things, he had a fire going and enough water to last until daylight. He thought about what he had seen earlier. Hallucinations are not unusual in these circumstances, he thought.

For some strange reason he remembered Mister Knaggs. Knaggs had been on a destroyer that was sunk in the Battle of Savo Island. He was small enough that the other sailors had pushed him through a porthole. Before he could put on his life jacket, he saw other sailors frantically swimming away from the ship, so he swam as he tried to call to the others for help. When he stopped and looked back, he saw his ship roll over and sink in less than a minute. It was just gone. There was no down suction because the water wasn't that deep there. Just some debris floating in the moonlight, marked the spot. He put on his life jacket and waited for the sharks, but by daylight a lifeboat found him, Knaggs said. Surface sailors would talk about the best place to be if the ship got hit. Larry always said the best place to be was on land, but that joke would only work once. Submariners didn't think that way. On a submarine, everybody was doomed to go down.

In the light of the fire, he gathered palm fronds and driftwood and using shoe strings and tearing his undershirt into strips, he managed to make himself a doubtful cot, but it would keep him off the sand while he slept. It worked like a marine's cot. You got yourself in the most comfortable position possible and you didn't move after that. He forced himself to go to sleep and when he got up, it was light.

The fire had gone out and the ashes were cold. He had a breakfast of chewing gum and drank the water in the bottle. He knew that it was imperative to scout the island. He had to find out if anybody lived on this island or came here regularly. He walked on the beach in a northward direction according to the sun. Having gone about a quarter mile, he came to a rivulet of freshwater, flowing across the sand and into the sea. He followed it upstream, but because of rocks and vegetation, he was unable to find its source. He thought about the waterborne pathogens that might be in the water, E.coli, Amoeba Proteus, Entamoeba Histolitica, the Cyclops that carried the larvae of Dracunulus Medinis and the Cercaria of other parasitic organisms. He would have to boil the water for five minutes, he figured. He looked in the intertidal sand for clam shells that were big enough to hold water and found nothing. He went further and found a large sandy point. He climbed to the top of the back dunes and looked around for any sign of life. Far out to the east there was a white boat. He was wishing that he had some way to signal it. Looking around, he saw that there weren't any large trees and the vegetation seemed to disappear inland. Looking for anything in the dunes, he found a broken board nearly buried in the sand. He pulled on it and it came out. Moving the sand had exposed the neck of a gallon jug. He pulled it out of the sand and looked at it. It must have been deposited there years ago by a storm. It had no cracks and Larry immediately realized that he could boil water in it. He took it to the sea and had the devil's own time trying to wash out the dirt and the dried algae but eventually he was satisfied with the job and took it back to the little rivulet and filled it with freshwater. Returning to his 'camp', he lit a fire and hung the jug over the flames, on a sturdy stick. After it had boiled long enough, he took the jug away from the fire and set it on the sand to cool then set it in the ocean to finish the job. He was ecstatic as he filled his water bottle then plugged the jug with what was left of his undershirt. Since he had water and being a well-fed person, his strength should last a couple days more, he figured. He thought about the boat he had seen. He had seen nothing from here, but local fishermen seem to come and go in his experience.

Even if he had had a thousand car tires to burn, he doubted that the boat he had seen would have come to investigate. At night, a fire would be much more likely to be noticed since the fishers would be keeping a watch so they didn't run aground.

Larry took his water bottle and walked southward on the beach. He thought about Montana back in Columbo. She talked about the great sand beaches they had. Sand was just dirt with good public relations. It was pretty but it didn't grow anything or yield anything. His granddaughter had said that if you're old, bald or ugly, you're outta' here, Larry recalled. Capability didn't mean anything except under these circumstances, apparently. When he got back to his camp, he saw a pelican snooping around and managed to kill it with a rock. He skinned and gutted it and cooked it over a fire. After he had eaten part of it, he laid down on his cot and slept for a few hours. Ever since he was a kid, he could wake up at any time that he wanted to, and he wanted to wake up at sunset.

When he woke up, it was still light, but the sun had gone down. He lit a fire and kept it small. He took off his shirt and selected the straightest stick he could find and pushed it through the arms then he wet the shirt in the sea. The air was perfectly still. The land breeze wouldn't start until later that night. As it started to get dark, he raised and lowered the shirt to send an SOS to any vessel out on the water. He did it for an hour then rested his arms for half an hour. He signaled again for an hour then sat down to rest, but he dozed off. When he woke up, he picked up his shirt and decided to wet it again. He dipped his shirt in the sea then pulled it out. He absently looked out to sea and was surprised to see a green running light, deck lights and a mast light. Assuming the mast light to be no more than thirty feet off the water, the vessel was about a half mile away and not moving. Running back to his 'camp', he hastily placed all his possessions and his shoes in his shirt and tied it tightly. He then tied his shirt to his belt in the back and went down to the water. The boat was still there. Larry hoped that they had anchored for the night. He walked into the water and started swimming in easy strokes. He didn't want to do too much splashing since sharks are an ever present danger in those waters. In fact he had no idea what could be out there and he prayed that there no jellyfish or any other nasty things. The water was ink black and he couldn't have seen a shark if it was six inches away. In ten minutes he was alongside the vessel, a fiberglass sailing yacht. He called out 'Ahoy' and waited for a reply but there was no movement or sound from the boat. He swam around to the stern and called out again, but there was still no answer. He climbed up the stern ladder and headed forward. When he got to the cabin, he untied his shirt and put his things back in his pockets and put his shoes and shirt on so he looked more presentable. The door to the cabin was open so he called out again. Getting no answer, he went to the bulkhead door. He heard Christina Aguillera singing in Spanish as he knocked on the door. He knocked again then receiving no reply, he opened the door. The compartment was filled with smoke and he called out the 'ahoy' as loud as he could. The festive scene of people laying around, drinking and smoking pot in a cloud while the music blared away, instantly dissolved into pandemonium as people yelled and screamed and tried to run and/or hide in the noisiest possible fashion. Somebody started yelling 'Policia', so Larry yelled 'No policia' as one of the young men tried to approach him. The man began yelling at the others to calm down, at least Larry hoped because he didn't recognize the language. After a minute the music was turned off and the pandemonium seemed to subside. He stood aside for two naked women who obviously wanted to get by. The man said something to him, so Larry said 'no comprendo' and removed the diplomatic chit from his shirt pocket and unfolded it and handed it to him. It was printed on a silk page and in a dozen languages said-I am an American national and I need assistance. My government will reward you for returning me to the nearest American post or consulate." Several international phone numbers were also listed. The fellow looked at it for a minute then said-'Nao falo ingles'. He turned and spoke to the couple people who were still present. A young woman in a night gown said something then went into the forward compartment. Another woman said something to the man and the man said something to him. Larry figured that they were asking how he got there, so he pantomined the sun passing through the sky twice then three of them in an airplane and the motor dying and the plane crashing into the sea and him swimming to the island and he pointed in the direction of the island. He did an impression of him looking out at the sea and seeing the boat and swimming to it. The people seemed to talk among themselves endlessly then finally the young woman emerged from the forward compartment with a girl no more than fifteen or sixteen. The girl looked down at the deck as the man talked to her. Larry thought that it was probably because there was some shame or legal problem with her being at a drug and booze orgy. The man said something.

"His name is Hector. He asks your name."

"Larry Mayer," Larry said happily.

She said something to Hector and he said something to her.

"Does he understand correctly that you were in an airplane crash two days ago?"

"Yes, Me, Tony Barber and Frank Elliot were flying to one of the islands when our engine quit and the plane crashed out there on the reef. I barely made it to the island. I never saw the others again," Larry explained.

The girl relayed his story to Hector and they had a little exchange before she spoke in English again.

"Hector would like you to show him this island," she said.

"Certainly, we'll have to go up on deck," Larry said.

The girl said something to Hector and he gestured to lead the way. When they got up on deck, Larry pointed out his signal fire as he spoke. He explained and gestured how he used his shirt to cover the fire in order to signal. The girl relayed what he told her and Hector spoke to her.

"Hector says that he didn't see the fire or signals when they anchored," the girl said.

He could have been firing sixteen inch guns and they wouldn't have noticed, Larry thought.

"I suppose that they would have to be looking this way to see it," Larry said.

The girl spoke to Hector and Hector spoke to her and gestured toward the island.

"Did you leave anything on the island?"

"No, I brought everything of value with me," Larry answered.

She spoke to Hector then Hector spoke to her again.

"Hector and Marie are from Portugal. They have friends here in the Canary Islands. The little islands around here are uninhabited. They come here to vacation because it is quiet here," she explained.

"Certainly, I am very happy that you were here."

"Hector will need to call on his phone and inform the Policia that he has found you here," the girl said.

"Let's do it," Larry said as he nodded happily.

When they went below, Larry showed Hector his driver's license. Hector and the girl went into the radio shack and the woman who seemed attached to Hector, motioned for him to come into the salon. Several of their friends were in there and they smiled at him. She indicated a variety of food prepared, so he made a sandwich with mutton and some sort of cheese. She gave him a glass of the dry red wine and Larry smiled and thanked her in Spanish. The girl came to him and asked for the number of the airplane so Larry wrote it down and handed it to her then she left.

For about twenty minutes, he tried to communicate with his saviors by drawing pictures, gesturing and making sounds that they could interpret. They seemed to be amused by him and the effort to reach them. He also noticed that many of the women seemed to be pretty unabashed about their clothing. They wore short gowns that did very little to hide their womanly charms, but Larry knew that this was common on island cultures like the Seychelles and even the Channel Islands. The girl and Hector came into the salon.

"Any luck? I mean did you get through to the authorities?" Larry asked.

The girl looked at the paper.

"The airplane of that number is missing from the airport, but there is no idea where it went. Nobody has found this Tony Barber, Frank Elliot or even your name," she said.

"Don't that beat all. Nobody was even looking for us," Larry remarked.

"The Policia ordered us to go to Puerto de Rosario so they can talk to you," the girl said.

"Certainly, can I have my Chit and my driver's license?"

"You must show them to the police," the girl said.

"I certainly will," Larry said.

She said something to Hector and Hector gave him back his license and chit. Hector asked that he stay below during the trip and he agreed to. Hector started the auxillary engine and another fellow helped bring up the anchor. He must think that I'm gonna' swim back to the island. It is strange that the 'authorities' he talked to didn't know anybody's name or had been alerted to an airplane missing. Some of these people weren't too swift. He could understand about wealthy people cruising out to the boondocks, as it were, to enjoy a weekend of debauchery. Even in the Canary Islands there were probably limits to things, but with all those Muslims crazies and Communists and god knows who else, bent on killing and destruction, let these people have their fun, Larry thought. Marie told him by pointing that the girls name was Josine. She had Josine translate as she asked questions. Larry explained about being married previously and having four children. He explained about being married last year and having a girl baby that was seven months old. He took out his wallet and showed the water damaged pictures to Marie. He really started missing home as he told Marie about it. He realized how lucky he was to have survived and be able to return home. Shirley would probably be upset enough when he told her about his ordeal. He would hold her and tell her that if he couldn't take a joke, he wouldn't have married her, he thought.

CHAPTER TEN

It was light by the time they reached Puerto de Rosario. As soon as the boat tied up, two policemen, short fellows, were waiting at the gangway. Instead of wearing their tropical uniform, they were in their dress blues with feather plumes. Their size might be a little understated, but certainly not their sense of style, Larry thought as one of them addressed him in English. He told him that they had a car and gestured in that direction, so Larry nodded and walked toward the car with them. He got in the back and they drove to the police station without talking. When they got to the station, one of the policemen opened to door for him and he thanked him as he got out. They escorted him into the building and left him at the office of a European looking man in a short sleeve shirt.

"I am Estancio Vargas. I am the Counsular Regulare for this island," he said, holding out his hand.

"I'm Larry Mayer," Larry said as they shook hands.

"Please sit down. Have some cold water. My information is that your airplane crashed in the sea near a small island almost three days ago and you were picked up by a boat belonging to Hector Hervanos of Lisbon. Is this so?"

"Well, I swam out to their boat in the darkness. I guess you could say that I found them," Larry said.

Vargas wrote something for a minute.

"From the telephone call, there were three men in the airplane. A Cessna 210, registration number NNSD7L. Is that correct?"

"Yes, there were."

"We did not get the names of the other two men."

"General Anthony Barber and Frank Elliot was the pilot," Larry replied.

He wrote again for a few minutes.

"Neither of them survived the crash?"

"They didn't make it to shore for sure. I didn't see them after I got out of the airplane. I barely made it myself," Larry said.

"And the cause of the crash?" he asked after a minute.

"Sudden engine failue. It just quit cold on us," Larry explained.

"No pilot error? Running out of gas or something similar?" he asked.

"We had more than half a tank. That was plenty of gas," Larry replied.

Vargas wrote for a few minutes then looked at Larry.

"My instructions are to have you flown to Gran Canaria. A member of the American Consulate will meet you there. The airplane will leave in one hour and twenty minutes. I will have someone take you to breakfast then take you to the airfield."

"Thank you. I am most grateful," Larry said.

"I am most happy to be of service," Vargas said as they shook hands.

A young woman came into the office."

"This is Evana," Vargas said.

He said something to her and she merely replied 'Si'.

"She doesn't speak English. Just follow her," Vargas said.

"Very good. Good-bye," Larry said then they left.

Evana took him right to the airfield and to a desk and handed a woman some paperwork and spoke to her for about five minutes then left. The woman, who spoke broken English, told him that her name was Mirra. She took him to a lounge and he got pancakes and sausage with coffee. He had only a couple Moroccan dirham in his wallet, but Mirra had got it on the house for him. She told him what gate and what airplane he would be flying in, but she didn't say much more than that. He asked her who he would be meeting and where he would be going. Each time she looked at him like he had asked an inappropriate question then answered that she didn't know. He would be flying on one of those high wing commuter planes, but Gran Canaria was the next island over and only about eighty miles away. Mirra handed the paperwork to the stewardess at the gate. The stewardess said something in Spanish and Mirra answered her then she nodded her head. Mirra stayed with him until he got on the plane.

They landed at the airport south of Las Palmas. Gran Canaria It was a much larger island in population and had a larger airport that could handle all but the biggest airliners. With typical Canarian efficiency, there was a driver holding a sign with his name as he came down the ramp. He had lost his luggage back in Morocco, so they could skip baggage claim. All he had was a plastic store bag with deodorant, tooth brush, tooth paste and shaving things. Surprisingly, even though a native, the consulate driver spoke excellent English and answered all the questions that he had. He had a small Mercedes sedan so Larry elected to sit in the front seat. Las Palmas was a big town and contained more than half of the islands 850,000 inhabitants. It was a sunny day and not too warm as they drove to the consulate. The city had the smell of flowers and spices as they went slowly through the streets crowded with pedestrians as much as cars. It seemed that the walkers didn't have any use for crosswalks or traffic signals. A large group would simply burst onto the street when the sidewalk could no longer contain them, Larry observed.

"No hurry here," the driver said in apparent anticipation of his question.

"Yes, certainly," Larry said.

He remembered that Marie had told him that half of the beaches were nude beaches and that seeing people in copulation was not uncommon on most of the islands. He had no intention of aggravating Shirley with any such foolishness, he thought. The car stopped in front of a two story white building and they got out and went inside. There was only one uniformed guard by the front desk. The man at the desk remained seated.

"This is Larry Mayer. He is to see the Envoy," the driver informed him.

"Do you have any identification," the man said, standing up, but not offering his hand.

Larry handed him his passport and his driver's license.

"I'll make a copy and run a 'make' through our data base," he said then he turned and walked down the hallway.

"This will not take long," the driver assured him.

Larry nodded his head and tried to smile. The closer to DC, the more anal the Embassy, goes the old saying.

"You are from Nantucket?" the driver asked.

"Yes, I am."

"I hope you like our island," he said.

"As far as weather, you got us beat all to hell," Larry said.

"It is good here. It rains for three or four months in the winter then no more rain until next winter."

"California is like that," Larry said.

"You have a wife?"

"She is my second wife. My first wife died four years ago now," Larry explained.

"My bambino is seven months old. A little boy," he said as he showed Larry a picture.

"Yes, he's a little cutie. Perhaps he can meet my daughter someday. She is seven months also," Larry said as he took out the picture of him holding her standing up.

"Holy mother, she is very beautiful," he remarked.

"All my children were very pretty as babies. Ornery as all get out. She gives her mother the 'whats for'."

"She is a great gift to you, senor."

"Yes, I'm sure that she is," Larry said.

They saw the man returning with an army officer.

"This is Lieutenant Colonel Samuel Butcher, the military attache'."

"Hello, I'm Larry Mayer," Larry said as they shook hands.

"Come with me, Mayer," Butcher said.

"Beg pardon, sir. I would like my driver's license and my passport returned," Larry requested.

"They will be returned before you leave. Come with me."

Everybody sounds like a cop nowadays, he thought. Think like a cop and act like an idiot. He just about had a bellyful of it already. They went into an office and Butcher motioned for him to sit down. This guy is a natural asshole. That uniform goes right through him, Larry thought as the light colonel tapped on his computer keys.

"I am restricted to only asking questions about your flights from Tangiers. Now, you say that you left Tangier in a Cessna 210 with General Anthony Barber and another man, Frank Elliot?"

"Yes, Elliot was the pilot," Larry added.

"Then you stopped at Agadir and refueled then flew westward over the ocean until the engine suddenly quit and the airplane went into the ocean in the vicinity of a small, uninhabited island in the Canary Island group?"

"I was told that it was an uninhabited island, yes."

"What was your destination?"

"I don't know. I wasn't told that. It should be on the flight plan."

"There was no flight plan and I don't believe that you don't know," he snapped.

"People who know me, never call me a liar. It is the pilot's job to file a flight plan, not mine."

"So you are so stupid to get on an airplane without knowing where it's going?" he asked incredulously.

"That happens sometimes in these 'spook' operations," Larry said.

"You said that Barber and Elliot died in the crash?"

"No, I said that I never saw them after I left the aircraft. It came down right in the breakers and was sinking rapidly, so I got out and swam for my life. They never made it to shore, but whether they died in the aircraft or made it out, I couldn't say."

"I don't believe anything you say," he snapped.

"Well that's too fucking bad, asshole. Since you don't, I guess that I can go now," Larry said, standing up.

"Sit down, Mayer!"

"I'm a civilian. I don't take orders from army asses. Never did in fact," Larry said.

He saw butcher go for his sidearm, so he grabbed for his right arm as he dived into him. As they went down, Larry got a hold of the 92F with his left hand. He raised it up and struck Butcher right in the face.

He struck him again in the side of the head then again in the forehead. Butcher was screaming for his life now and several men came in as Larry lambasted him one more time. They grabbed his arms and pulled Larry off of him.

"Don't you ever pull a pistol on me you son of a bitch. I'll kill you with it next time," Larry yelled at him as they dragged him out of the room. They took Larry to another room and left him there. He heard a commotion in the hallway for a few minutes then things calmed down, it seemed. An hour later, a man came into the room alone and identified himself as the Domestic Envoy, Kyle Rothmann, in a West Virginia accent.

"Well, there has been quite a little bit of trouble here. We got a communication to leave you alone pending further instructions. Butcher has several serious head injuries. You must have beat the West Point outta' him," he quipped.

"It would take somewhat more than that," Larry stated.

"We can't get a clear read on you. We have had several top level requests to account for Barber. I just talked to a Turnbull from the State Department. He was madder than you, if you can believe it. I told him that Barber is gone. Buried at sea, apparently. He's gonna' have to get over it."

"I've known Turnbull for years. Every time I've run into him, I wished I hadn't."

"I have no reason to doubt anything you say. Barber sleeps with the fishes," the Envoy said.

"I did a job in Sri Lanka. That was supposed to be the end of it, but I had to go to Bangkok then to Vietnam. I told that idiot, Barber that I was done. I was pulling out. I ended up retrieving some 'friends' for the CIA in Morocco and Barber shows up there again. This was supposed to be the jumping off point for home. Next stop, Nantucket Island, the Reds, lightship baskets, windmills, exorbitant taxes. I don't need assholes like Butcher trying to fuck over me. I've had a bellyful of it already," Larry snapped.

"Yes, doubtless you probably need to recuperate after your ordeal. That's understandable, certainly," he said.

"I would like to talk to my wife," Larry requested.

"I'll see what I can do. Is there anything else you need?"

"A comfortable bed to sleep in."

"Certainly we can get you that. I'll be back in a half hour or less," Rothmann said then he left.

Larry sat in an overstuffed recliner and tried to relax. At least the Envoy seemed understanding and acted like he was trying to be helpful. In ten minutes he returned.

"I got permission for you to call home. You can't mention anything about the operation or any names. The operation is still classified as Top Secret."

"Great, where's the overseas line?"

"You can use this phone," the Envoy said as he picked it up and dialed the four digit overseas number for America then handed the phone to Larry. Larry dialed their home phone.

"Mayer residence, Rosa."

"Rosa, this is Larry. Is Shirley there?"

"Larry, holy mother of God! Shirley has been worried to death about you!"

"Is she there?"

"She is outside. I will call her...Here she is, senor."

Smiling and nodding, she handed the phone to Shirley.

"Larry!" she exclaimed.

"Hi, Baby love. I wanted to give you a call..."

"Where the hell are you, Larry!?"

"In the Canary islands, of all places-"

"What the hell's going on! Five days ago I got a telegram that you were safe in the US embassy in Bangkok. When I finally got through to them, they said that you had left."

"Yeah, it's kind of a funny story that's classified at the moment but I'm safe here on Gran Canaria. A place called Las Palmas. It's a pretty place. The weather is great..."

"How did you get there again?"

"Well, we flew out here in a Cessna, but we came up a little short on the runway."

"How short?"

"Oh, seventy or eighty miles, I guess."

"I must not have heard you right. Say again," she requested.

"There was a little accident, but I'm fine. Don't worry, Baby, I'm coming home in one piece," Larry assured her.

"Oh my god! How can you tell me not to worry?" Shirley exclaimed. By her voice, she was ready to cry. Larry had to control himself and keep his voice normal.

"It's okay, Sweetie. How's the baby doing?"

"She's sleeping now. She has two lower teeth now. I keep telling her that daddy will be home."

"Well, you keep telling her that because I am coming home. My bags got lost. I didn't have time to buy you anything in Thailand or Morocco. I'll probably buy another suitcase here. I'm carrying my deodorant and toothpaste in a plastic bag. I'll try to buy you and Ally something while I'm here. I'll have to put it on the charge card."

"The only thing I want is to see is you coming up our walkway!"

"Sure thing! I'll take Sandpiper Air," Larry quipped.

"I'll come get you in Boston or hell if I have to!"

"Now that's a navy wife! Alright, Baby, I'll let you know when I'm coming."

"I miss you so much. I'm so happy to hear from you."

"Save the tears for when I get home, Sweetie. Tell Ally that Daddy will get those big fat baby cheeks as soon as I see her."

"I will. I'll tell her that daddy is on his way home."

"I miss you too. I'll tell you how much when we're together again. My time is up. I love you. Bye bye Baby."

"I love you, Larry. Bye," Shirley said then Larry hung up the phone.

After the phone call, the Envoy returned.

"How are things at home?"

"It seemed a lot easier in the old days," Larry said.

"Yes, I suppose it was. We're still burning up the wires here. No telling when we can get clearance to send you home."

"I can't go home. I have to make one more stop. I have an address and phone number in Salzburg that I have to check out."

"If you leave here, we can't help you. You're on your own."

"If you could get me on the soonest flight there, that would be a big help," Larry said.

"There is a flight to Madrid in two hours. You should be able to get a flight to Vienna then drive to Salzburg."

"That would be great. Can you check on it for me?"

"Sure, I'll get you a car. We'll get you there the fastest way we can," Rothmann assured him.

After Larry left the embassy, Rothmann informed the embassy in Madrid via the diplomatic burst encoder, that Larry would be stopping there on his way to Vienna. Unbeknownst to Larry, his location was being monitored. Only a handful of people even knew why.

CHAPTER ELEVEN

When he arrived in Vienna, he showed them his passport. When they asked about his bags, he told them that they were lost. They asked where he was going, and he told them the name and address of a hotel in Salzburg. He was able to rent a car at the airport and drive to Salzburg. When he arrived at the hotel and checked in, they gave him a message to call a fellow named Klaus and the phone number.

The next morning he drove to the farm of an old acquaintance that did work on cars and motorcycles. Otto was a mechanical genius. The kind of guy that could and had made his own machine tools. In the past, he had also been involved in gun 'alterations' and making 'special guns' for questionable purposes. He had made a gun that could make a two inch hole in the bottom of a ship. A diver could use it without any harm from concussion. The navy wasn't interested, but Larry convinced an Admiral to buy the proprietary rights to it for future use. Larry heard the sound of an engine and propeller coming from behind a Quonset hut. Walking around the hut, he saw Otto bent over and looking at the engine of a small helicopter, called a Skylark, in America. The man looked at him then backed away from the helicopter while remaining stooped down because the rotor blades were turning.

"Otto, you old draft dodger. How the hell you doing?" Larry asked as they shook hands.

"I can't complain, Herr Mayer. How do you like my new machine?"

"My wife is the helicopter pilot, I'm afraid. This isn't your usual line of business," Larry said.

"I did some race car work for the son of a driver. He couldn't pay me, so he gave me this machine in parts. I have completed the assembly and have checked the engine. You are still a pilot, not so?"

"Let's see what you have here," Larry said.

He was glad that he had a few hours of instruction with Shirley in a dual control helicopter. They both stooped and approached the helicopter.

The nineteen foot main rotor was seven feet from the ground and it and the tail rotor were controlled by rigid push-pull controls. Larry got in the seat and put on the seat belt. He gave the okay signal to Otto and Otto backed away. Larry twisted the grip on the collective stick to rev the Rotax 582 engine. He held the engine and rotor rpm on the high end of the green then raised the collective stick slowly to increase the pitch. He could hear the blades slapping air and the helicopter slowly lifted off the ground. He held it at five feet for a minute and looked around and listened for anything unusual. Satisfied, he raised the collective slightly and went to twelve feet. After hovering for another minute, he pushed the cyclic stick forward and the helicopter went forward. He pulled it back and the helicopter stopped. He went up to thirty feet then pushed the cyclic stick forward again and flew to the edge of the field. He pushed the stick left while holding it forward and it turned left. He brought it around and put the stick back in the middle. Unlike an airplane, you held the cyclic stick over constantly while turning and similarly, you didn't have to bank and steer in the opposite direction to straighten it up. Putting the cyclic stick back in the center straightened it out, like a car. He flew back to where he started, spun it around then hovered and brought it down by reducing collective pitch and then the throttle. When he landed, he reduced the engine to an idle then shutdown the magneto. Otto came running out to him.

"I had to use a little much left pedal when flying. Adjust that linkage and it should be okay," Larry said as he unbuckled his seat belt.

"Yes, I will do that. That was good flying. Thank you," Otto said.

"No problem, old buddy."

Inside, Helga brought them red wine and venison with potatoes. After she served them, she left the room.

"I have been working on a problem. Somebody made a kill with a .357 mag but nobody in the next room or the hallway heard anything. Have you ever heard of that?" Larry asked.

"On the best job, there is a pop like opening a bottle of wine. Nobody hears anything because nobody recognizes it as a firearm being discharged. You see, if you are close enough, the supersonic crack doesn't develop and if the suppressor is good enough, it sounds like the wine bottle again. Revolvers have leakage between the chamber and the barrel, so that is no good. There are .357 automatics, but the heavy suppressor must move with the barrel. I did a job using your T/C Contender single shot in .357. It was the best pistol for that kind of job. Are you working for the police?"

"No, it was a relative of a friend of the wife. I'm just asking around as a favor."

"There was talk of an assassination attempt on a high ranking official of your government. This was to take place in the far east. The triggerman was shot while sleeping. This was in Sri Lanka, I heard. Does this sound like your business?" Otto asked.

"No, but it sounds like somebody's business. Sri Lanka is a crazy place. I never go there. This fellow bought the farm in Morocco," Larry lied.

"Morocco was good in the old days. Good money and people let you to do your business, then the drug people came in and the political terrorists came with them."

"Can you tell me the name of the guy in Sri Lanka, so I can cross him off my list?"

"Stumpfel, Hans Stumpfel was his real name. He was our age. One of the best guys in that business. He was also known as Friederick Mercanne and Dieter Kleist. You know that these types have identity papers, drivers license and passports in several names that they can identify themselves with." Otto stated.

"In those days, I didn't need a name. I did it for God and country."

"God does not pay at all and the country does not pay much," Otto remarked.

"A congressional medal of honor is ten dollars a month, but you gotta' be sixty five to collect."

"I think I will ask for 100,000 schilling for the Furia. That is 20,000 US dollars. That is a good price, I think."

"The kit price is $20,000, so that is a good price for one that is ready to fly," Larry agreed.

"So what is it that you do now?"

"Absolutely nothing. The wife has all the money we need."

"That does not sound like you," Otto said, looking puzzled.

"I do a lot more diving. I haven't been too successful in treasure hunting. I found some stuff in the Florida Keys. Nothing around Nantucket. I just came from the Canary Islands."

"A fellow found a considerable pirate treasure in Cape Cod. That is your area?" Otto asked.

"Yes, he had been looking for twenty years. Everybody tells me where there is a treasure, but I never find it where they say it is."

"Sometime we should look together. I think that we could do well working together."

"Yes, certainly. I'll let you know if there is an opportunity to do that," Larry said.

When Larry returned to his hotel in Salzburg, there was a message to meet the Klaus that he had tried to contact earlier, in an alley off of Karlstrasse. Since it was drizzling, he borrowed a raincoat from the hotel and put the little HsC Mauser in the pocket.

Larry waited in the alley as he had been instructed. The drizzle was steadily getting worse. He waited next to the building where the rain wasn't as bad. Right on time, he saw the headlights of a small Mercedes as it turned into the alley and stopped. The engine was left running and the lights left on. The door opened and the driver got out. He could not see him clearly until he came in front of the car then he was a her. She was young, had long dark hair and wearing a trench coat. Larry stopped several feet away, but she was European so she came right up to him.

"I could kill you now," she said.

"That doesn't seem to be your style. I heard that you killed old Hans."

"Hans was sent to kill an official of your government and I was sent to stop Hans."

"That sort of discourages others with the same idea, I suppose. I'm surprised he wasn't more careful," Larry said.

"Perhaps you can see that an attractive young woman can gain access by claiming to be a friend."

"Yes, you certainly can pull off that ruse," Larry said.

"I heard a rumor that you were being fooled. It was a cover for the assassination attempt."

"That figures. None of the pieces ever seemed to fit."

"I ask that you will say nothing of this meeting for twenty four hours."

"Since you leave me in peace, I will say nothing about this meeting to anyone, ever."

"You are an honorable man, Herr Mayer," she said then she turned and walked back to her car, got in and backed out and was gone.

Larry thought about what she had said then he wondered at what she had done. She turned her back to him and went back to her car. Did she think that he was incapable of shooting someone in the back? Did she know that he wasn't inclined to shoot anybody unless he had a reason and his only reason now would be if there was an immediate danger to his life? One never knew about hired killers, if indeed she was one. He thought about people like young Virginia, in Columbo, who thought that he was no better than a hit man or a psychotic terrorist. Sure, let's tell the Hitlers and Tojos of the world that we're very sorry for the misunderstanding and the behavior of George W. Bush. What the hell are we fighting for? That is the silliest mother fucking question that he ever heard. An army question, for sure. A question asked by somebody who has already made up their mind not to fight. He wouldn't have somebody like that on his mission or even on his ship if he could help it. Not getting your ass, or your team, shot up all to hell is all that you had to worry about.

Having no reason to stay in Europe, he caught a plane to Madrid. In Madrid, he would catch a plane to Boston. He bought luggage and a few things before he left Madrid. He wanted to bring back something tangible.

CHAPTER TWELVE

Shirley met him as he came through customs. He set his bags down as she ran up to him and embraced him like she would never let go. His whole body shook then he relaxed in her grip. He had his eyes closed and he didn't think about what other people thought.

"Bloody newlyweds," a man said in a British accent as he passed by them.

Shirley began to cry with joy and Larry had to choke back the tears. He thought somebody would tell them to move on after five minutes.

"I lost my bags, so I had to buy new ones in Madrid. I bought some things for the four of you."

"Lets go," Shirley said as she grabbed a suitcase. They walked out of the ground level door and Shirley had her Beechcraft parked in the usual place.

"Fall is definitely here. I told Barber that a month ago. It seems like a thousand years ago now."

"I can't wait to get you home. After you left, I talked with Amy and Christine. They really appreciated you getting her out of prison. They wanted to come for Thanksgiving and tell you in person."

"I don't think I'll ever do it again. Everybody thought I got paid a million dollars. Nobody believed that I did it for free," Larry said as he opened the 'cargo door' on the Beechcraft. They put his luggage in the plane then they did the preflight and Shirley flew them home. Larry said nothing about the operation because he didn't want to upset Shirley at that time. He would have to tell her later, but for now he tried to enjoy the time together. When they came through the front door, Rosa, Olga and the baby were there to greet them. The hugs and tears seemed to go on forever. Larry had bought Rosa a festival outfit similar to the ones he had seen in the Canary Islands. He gave Olga a reproduction of a Faberge egg and he gave Shirley a gold chain with locket which Marie had given him.

"I'll tell you how I got that, later," Larry said then he gave Althea an ornate bean rattle which had been made in the Canary Islands.

They had a great dinner then Shirley and Larry drove around the island to be alone. They stopped at the beach that Barber had taken him to.

"The weather on the Canary Islands is just great. It's like southern California before it was ruined," Larry said then he was quiet.

"There's something you want to tell me?"

"No infidelity...don't worry about that. After several misadventures in Bangkok and Vietnam, I was headed back home. I ran into Brown and McLeod in Morocco. I whacked a couple more dudes there then Barber shows up with a Cessna 210 and a pilot named Frank Elliot. We flew from Tangiers to Agadir on the Atlantic coast then we headed to the Canaries. I guess we were headed that way, because I was not told where we were going. Anyway, the engine quit cold and we went down on this reef. I got the hell out, but I never saw Barber or Elliot again. I swam to this small, uninhabited island with nothing but an empty water bottle. During the two days I was there, I managed to get enough water and kill a pelican for food. I was trying to signal when I saw the lights of a sailing yacht. I swam to the yacht in the utter darkness and tried to call to them, but nobody answered. I went onboard and found them in the middle of a booze/drug orgy. You should have seen the smoke. All the women start screaming and running all over the place and yelling 'Policia', so I'm yelling 'No Policia'. Just about everybody was naked or close to it. Just utter pandemonium. Finally the owner, Hector, gets the music shut off, but this guy knows no English, so it takes about ten minutes to get this girl, who's only about fifteen, to translate. Meanwhile, I'm trying to communicate with this woman, Marie, who is the wife of the owner, by drawing and gesticulating and making sounds. Well, they bring out this girl and she translates for me, but Hector doesn't believe me for some reason. I have to go topside with him and show him the island and my signal fire, which is still burning. So he calls on his maritime radio and all they can tell him is that the airplane is missing from the airfield, but they never heard of Tony Barber, Frank Elliot or me. Hector is told to turn me over to the authorities, which is fine with me. So this woman, Marie, is very hospitable and using the girl, I tell her about you and Althea. She tells me that you two are a great gift to me and she gave me that chain to give to you," Larry concluded.

"You could have died in the crash, in the water or on that island! I'm so sorry I got you into all of that mess," she said, grabbing his arm.

"If I couldn't take a joke, I wouldn't have married you," Larry quipped.

"That old Mickey Mouse-Chicken Shit doesn't apply here," Shirley stated then they kissed again.

"We should go to Gran Canaria. Most of the beaches there are nude. You get men and women together and nude, you know what happens?"

"I can imagine," Shirley replied.

"If the beach isn't crowded, they just do their business right on the sand. They expect nobody to bother them. Craziest thing you have ever seen."

"I was there years ago when there were even less people. They relax the laws about that to get people to come there and spend money. There's no gay community, but sometimes you see same sex couples also," Shirley added.

"There must have been four hundred women, all wearing costumes like I gave Rosa. Very festive."

"So you had to kill a couple guys in Morocco?" she asked.

"I was in Vietnam and I got the hell outta' there and returned to Bangkok. Barber puts me in the Sugi Fora hotel and later these three punks are coming down the hallway, whipping out their butterfly knives, so I killed them with a Mark 3 pistol and got myself to the embassy. That is when they sent you the message. I ended up flying to New Delhi then to Morocco. I went with Brown to an airfield at Meknes. We pursued some terrorist in a helicopter. They had McLeod tied and gagged, so I shot one while flying this old Twin Cherokee then I rammed their tail rotor and forced them down at an old airfield near Tetouan. I shot two of them there then we flew to an airfield at Tangiers which was a safe haven for the CIA. I ran into Barber there and I've already told you about the Cessna."

"Plenty of women in all those places?" she asked.

"Funny you should mention that. Before the big dive, me and my Top man, Scott, got invited to a reception at the consulate in Columbo. Scott introduced me to these three young women, Virginia, Montana and Dakota. Montana came to my room later to ask about diving in the ocean there. I told her that I probably wouldn't have the opportunity to dive while there," Larry explained.

"Anything else?" she asked.

"Yeah, but I explained to her about you and Ally. I'm afraid that I embarrassed her."

"Can't blame a girl for trying, I guess," Shirley remarked.

"Very nice young ladies. I can't say that about the Envoy. He was slamming me and my ability in no uncertain terms. A fucker who never dived in his life! Can you imagine that?"

"I imagine you set him straight."

"I wrang out his tie while he was still wearing it," Larry said.

"Any other attacks on embassy personnel?" she asked.

"A light colonel, the Military Attache' in Las Palmas. He tried the 'tough cop' routine on me, so I did the 'pistol whipping the asshole' routine on him. Not enough to get the 'West Point' out of him though," Larry replied.

"I'm keeping you at home from now on, guy," Shirley stated.

"It doesn't seem like such an ordeal now. Just another Sunday cookout story."

"Are you kidding! There were at least five circumstances in which you could have been killed!" Shirley exclaimed.

Larry was happy that she appreciated that fact.

"If it was gonna' be easy, they wouldn't have let young Christine out of jail, I suppose," Larry said.

"I swear to god that I won't put you in a situation like that again," Shirley stated.

"In this life, you try to keep paddling your canoe in the right direction. That's all either of us can do."

"I won't volunteer you to sweep the walkway," Shirley assured him.

He held on to her tightly. She felt so good as they embraced. He thought about those words from 'A Groovy Kind of Love'.

"It will be great to sleep on my own bed tonight."

"It is so good having you back. I can stop lying in bed, worrying about you."

"But you're so ornery!"

"You know what to do about that," Shirley said then they kissed again.

"But the baby will be so bad. Just like her mother," Larry quipped.

"We will try to be a great gift to you," Shirley assured him.

"That doesn't sound too hard. You always have been."

CHAPTER THIRTEEN

The telephone rang and Rosa answered it.

"Larry, the phone is for you," she said.

"Thank you, Rosa," Larry said as he took the phone from her.

"Mayer speaking," he said.

"This is Agent Harrison, FBI. Mister Mayer, what does the number 1097366 mean to you?"

"That is the serial number of the M14 rifle that I had years ago in the Navy."

"That is correct. I had to verify your identity. It is imperative that I talk to you as soon as possible."

"I suppose you want me to go to DC or something. I really don't feel up to traveling right now," Larry said.

"I am on the island. I will come to see you. When will you be available?"

"Well, since you're being so accommodating, you can stop by anytime," Larry replied.

"Six o'clock this evening?"

"Sure, we can have supper outta' the way by then. Just knock on the door."

"I'll see you then," Harrison said.

"Good-bye," Larry said.

When he hung up the phone, Shirley was looking at him.

"FBI Agent Harrison is stopping by."

"What for?" she asked.

"He said, to arrest you for treating me so bad," Larry said as he embraced her.

"The neighbors already think we're 'Mister and Misses Smith' and this isn't helping," she said.

"Does getting someone out of prison by doing the government a favor, violate any laws?"

"What about all the other things that happened?" Shirley asked.

"That was overseas. They ain't got any jurisdiction over that," Larry said.

"We'll have to wait and see what he wants. Do you want me with you?"

"No, not unless he asks for you to corroborate something. I think it will be okay," Larry said.

Agent Harrison showed up promptly at six o'clock and showed his badge and Larry let him in. Larry remembered the rumors about people from other government agencies posing as FBI agents. Supposedly that practice had been stopped, but in the Obama administration, who knew. They went to the dining room because the table was bigger in there. Harrison asked how many people were living in the house, so Larry told him. Rosa brought them coffee as Harrison opened his brief case.

"We haven't received all of the information as yet. Right now, our inquiry is focused on the death of General Anthony Barber. I must tell you that there could be criminal charges for misuse of government money. Do you understand this?"

"Well Harrison, I didn't get any money for doing anything I did. I did it to get a relative of a friend out of prison. I had to use the bank card a lot, so poor Shirley ended up paying for a lot of my expenses. I never handled money for anybody either."

"According to the information we have, Anthony Barber died in a plane crash eight days ago at approximately 2:05 local time in the Canary

Islands. This information was supplied by you to the local police and to US embassy officials on Gran Canaria. Do you still maintain this to be true?"

"Yes, I do. Whether he made it out of the airplane or not, I couldn't say, but he certainly didn't make it to the shore. Him and the pilot, Frank Elliot, died out there somewhere," Larry stated.

He wrote for a while and Larry knew that he had a recorder hidden in his brief case.

"Can you summarize why and how you came to be in an airplane with General Barber?"

"Yes, I ran into General Barber at the airport just outside of Tangiers. This was approximately 0600..."

"Excuse me, why were you at that airport?"

"I had flown in the previous evening in an old Twin Cherokee with two guys, Harold Brown and Tyrone McLeod. Barber called me there about a half hour after I arrived and told me that he would meet me there at 0600 the next morning."

He wrote some more then looked at Larry.

"Go on."

"He took me out to a Cessna 210, registration number November November Sierra Delta seven Lima, and introduced me to the pilot, Frank Elliot. They were ready to go and I had lost my luggage earlier, so we took off almost immediately. We flew southwest to Agadir and landed and refueled there. We ate there also. We left the airfield for about a half hour. I guess we were there for an hour and a half altogether. Barber never told me where we were going. All he ever told me was that we would eventually make it back to here. Elliot took us out over the ocean, so I figured that we were going to the Canaries since it's the only thing out there. Barber didn't say too much about our business, but I figured that that was because Elliot was not in on the operation. I saw some smaller islands in front of us. Barber told me that the smaller islands were not inhabited then the engine quit cold on us and we went down. Elliot held it straight and level all the way down. He did a good job of that. Right before we hit the water,

I unlatched the door and held it ajar with my right arm and foot. When we stopped, I forced the door open, got out and started swimming for my life. We were in the surf line, so it was a tough place to be. When I was clear of the breakers, I turned and looked, but I didn't see anything. No one in the water and no airplane. I kept swimming and got to the island. I had to survive for two days on my wits then I saw a boat and swam out to it."

Harrison didn't act like he was interested in any heroic stories of survival.

"Did Barber have anything in the airplane? Any luggage?"

"To be honest, I couldn't tell ya'. That would have been in the back and I always sat in the front. In fact, Barber had always told me to sit in the front," Larry replied.

Harrison wrote some more.

"Going back to the beginning in order to clarify a few things. You said that Barber called you about half an hour after you landed at the airport near Tangiers. Did you have a cell phone?"

"No, he called me on one of the phones at the airport."

"How did he know you were there?"

"I can neither confirm or deny that the CIA conduct operations from that airfield," Larry replied.

"So you think that somebody informed him that you were there?"

"That's the only thing I can think of."

"He was carrying money with him. We would like to recover that money if we can. Can you give us the location?"

So, that's the only value to that sucker's life now, Larry thought.

"Sure, I'll draw you a map," Larry said.

He had written down the GPS numbers of the yacht at anchor, on the back of his Triple-A card. The yacht was approximately a half mile offshore and the reef, where the plane had crashed, was halfway between them. This line was almost east-west. Hector had verified the direction and distances when they were up on deck that night. Using a sharpie and a pen, he drew a map that anybody could read. He gave the map to Harrison. He looked at it for a moment.

"You say that you swam out to the yacht in the dark after being on the island for two days?"

"Yes, I did."

"Didn't you state earlier that you had difficulty making it to the shore from the crash site, which was half that distance?"

"Yes, I'm glad that you appreciate that fact. When there is a large landmass like the continent of Africa and it's cooling down, the wind blows shoreward, so the waves that I had to deal with earlier were no longer coming over the reef. The water was calm for a while, fortunately," Larry replied.

"After you boarded the yacht, where did you go?"

"They took me to Puerto de Rosario where the police turned me over to the Consulate Regular, a guy named Vargas. He arranged for me to be flown to Las Palmas on Gran Canaria, where I was taken to our consulate. I left there on my own and went to Madrid, then to Vienna and Salzburg then back to Madrid then to Boston and here," Larry stated.

"Why did you go to Vienna and Salzburg?" he asked.

"I was looking up an old friend," he replied.

"And your friends name?"

"Otto Keller."

"And your business with Herr Keller?"

"I was checking out a helicopter that he had built himself. He is an inventor of things," Larry replied.

"How did you pay for all this travel?"

"Since leaving our consulate in Las Palmas, I traveled on Shirley's bank card. Poor Shirley is footing the bill here," Larry said.

"All the time that you were associated with General Barber, he never mentioned anything about money?"

"No, we never talked about money, for sure."

"Did you have any other contact in this operation?"

"Initially Admiral Harvey Turnbull contacted me. I told him that I wasn't interested then General Barber contacted me."

"Did you have any more contact with Harvey Turnbull?"

"No, I didn't. I don't know what his role was in the operation, but I'm sure that he was working with Barber."

"Very good. I'll pass on this information and hopefully we can get this matter resolved," Harrison said as he put things back in his briefcase.

Larry went to the door with him.

"Nice meeting you. Stop back again sometime," Larry said, shaking his hand.

Two days later, Harrison came back and informed Shirley that Navy helicopters had spotted the airplane at low tide, exactly where Larry had said it was. Larry knew that any decent sized helicopter could lift the Cessna. All it would take is a couple divers to get slings under the wings and/or fuselage, and it could be flown to the nearest auxillary or aircraft carrier. Doubtless this had already been done, Larry thought. The government wouldn't have informed him until the recovery was successfully completed. He had left his bags back in Meknes, so he didn't have any claims for recovered property. Except for a dark suit and work clothes he brought, he had been given utilities and service khakis for a chief. Something that he could find in any Army surplus store, he thought.

CHAPTER FOURTEEN

Larry was visiting Joe's grave in Glendale cemetery. He was walking up the road when he saw a bummy looking guy coming toward him.

"Mayer, I thought you was dead."

"Crazy Jack! How in the hell are ya'?"

"You know that you eat nearly a ton of food a year. Think of all the food that would save."

"You gotta' stay on the meds, old buddy."

"Medication! They were poisoning me. I have to pick up aluminum cans, but I'm free of those bastards."

"They kinda' resented it when you talked about killing Obama. You can't do that on Facebook."

"It's too late now. The federal deficit is way over the limit. A civil war is inevitable," Jack said.

"I'm looking for another country to live in."

"Martha's Vineyard ain't gonna' do it."

"Nantucket," Larry corrected him.

"I like California. It was always warm. I have to sleep outside a lot."

'Yeah, that's rough, but that's probably where any war would start."

"I got broke inside. I told them I was broke inside. Captain Bowers and them others wouldn't hear me. They said that you were still in the game and what was wrong with me. Assholes who ain't anywhere near the shooting asking what the hell's wrong with me!!"

"They pulled you out and sent you to detox," Larry reminded him.

"They didn't understand. We needed drugs or alcohol to deal with it every day. To deal with that shit every day."

"I told you and everybody else that you will end up with an addiction to something and you won't be able to get outta' bed in the morning. I made that perfectly clear," Larry said.

"Don't be looking to apologize at the hour of my death."

"Gotcha', hold the repentance."

Crazy Jack looked at him for a minute.

"Somebody's gotta' take responsibility. You didn't go out that day. You wouldn't go out that day!"

"The operation was for the next day. I wouldn't have some son of a bitch balling up the operation by changing the planning to make himself look good. You guys got chopped to shit and we did it the next day as planned without a hitch. I chewed some ass for that, you can bet."

"It was your fault! You have to take responsibility!" Crazy Jack shouted as he lunged at Larry.

Larry landed a kick in his stomach, knocking the wind out of him.

"Now get this in your confused head, it was Captain Turnbull who sent you. I had nothing to do with it. I remember you guys having your little joke about me being afraid. With you wounded and the rest killed, I hope you enjoyed your little laugh," Larry snapped.

"Chief Cole is over there. Somebody puts flowers on his grave every day," Jack said after a minute.

"I found his airplane on the bottom of the ocean," Larry informed him.

"He was my instructor. He always said-'One stiff more or less. Nobody will notice."

Larry knew that that was Haroldson.

"I've already said good-bye," Jack said.

"Alright," Larry said.

"This is a nice place for a hero to rest."

Larry didn't like the way he sounded, but he walked over to Joe's grave. After a minute, he turned around and saw Jack lying face down, at the side of the road. He went back and looked at him. He was non-responsive and there was a syringe next to him. He called 911 and waited for the Police and the EMS. He told them that he knew nothing about the man. He told them that he was visiting the grave of an old navy buddy. He showed them his Massachusetts driver's license. He didn't want to get involved because he didn't know what getting involved entailed. He had learned a hard lesson about that.

"This happens all the time," the policeman assured him as they were putting the body in the EMS van.

"I've never seen it happen on Nantucket."

"I wish I could live there," the policeman said.

"Lost dogs are a big problem."

"It sounds like paradise," he said, smiling.

As Larry was walking back to his car, he thought about the last time he had served together with Joe and 'Hard Ass' Haroldson.

Larry and Joe were sitting at the meeting table in the Chiefs' Quarters when Senior Chief Haroldson came in.

"Good morning, Senior Chief."

"How's it going, guys," he said as he went over to the coffee pot.

"I can't complain," Larry said.

"Nobody will listen anyway," Haroldson said.

"My parents always said-'Nobody but God and he don't like complainers'. Here's the files on the new guys," Larry said, indicating the five folders on the table.

"They're all from New London?"

"These five are from Mare's Island," Larry replied.

"Damn, send me back to New London," the Senior Chief said.

"Where the sun keeps shinin' through the pouring rain..." Joe sang.

"You're gonna' leave me alone with this faggot. Where you going?"

"I'm takin' the wife and kids to Disney World."

"You rob a bank?" Haroldson asked.

"I won the tickets in the NCO's drawing."

"He had to feel-up the bitch to get the tickets outta' her," Joe quipped.

"When I told her it was six tickets, she nearly had a heart'astroke."

"See, if it was me, it would have been only one ticket then I could have sold it and not missed any duty time," Haroldson said.

"Put a crowbar in your wallet and pry out five dollars next time, tightwad."

"You don't wanna' go the Disney World. It a well known fact that Walt Disney hated children," Haroldson said.

"It's a fact that I ain't getting' outta' this trip," Larry said.

"Sorry guys, your instructor couldn't be here today because he's a miserable panty waist."

"Who is enjoying himself at Disney World," Larry added.

"I think he's gonna' pull a Buster Seavers on us," Joe joked.

"I put his sea bag in his car. He says-'I think I'm gonna' go home and kill my wife.' I said-'Okay, see ya' Monday'." When the CID asked me, I told them that he didn't say anything unusual," Larry said.

"Yeah, he said that he was going home and killing his wife. Naturally there was nothing about that statement that would lead you to believe that he would empty his forty five into his wife then kill himself," Haroldson said.

"Some guys talk shit all the time. They would never do anything like that."

"You were the last person on the base that he talked to. They would have hung you out to dry. You would be saluting the Philipino Mess stewards because of something you had absolutely no involvement in," Haroldson maintained.

How true, Larry thought as he got in his car. He drove through the cemetery gates and turned south, toward the airport. At Logan, he heard a PA announcement for Larry Mayer to report to the FAA office. He went to the information desk and a man in an overcoat walked up to him.

"I'll take this, Jan. Come with me, Larry," he said.

Larry was feeling apprehensive and didn't move.

"What's this about? Who are you?"

"You know me as Smith," he said, smiling.

"I ain't goin' anywhere with you, Smith."

"I can understand your reluctance. This is a debriefing, in fact."

"You can talk all you want, but I'm not believing any of it and I've had a bellyful of you and your friends," Larry snapped.

"We'll just be in that little room over there. You can search me for weapons if you like."

Larry looked at him for a moment.

"You have an hour and ten minutes before your plane leaves. I'll hold it for you if necessary."

"Alright," Larry agreed.

Smith took him to the little office then took him through another door behind the office where there was a small conference room.

"Sit down there if you like. You have an unusual style, but who am I to complain. I was the one that got Christine Bell out of prison. You should probably get more compensation than that. Coffee?"

"No thanks. Smith, it seems like I remember hearing about a fellow named Jones. This sounds like a TV series," Larry remarked.

"You convinced Harrison. I talked to Brown and the FBI director, myself. No one had a bad word to say about you. They were talking about giving you a reward. You can report the expenses on your bank card. Is there anything else to report?"

"Well, there's the valued added thing," Larry wisecracked.

Smith poured himself a cup then sat down. He took something out of his pocket and handed it to Larry.

"Do you recognize him?" Smith asked, showing him a pilot's license.

"Yes, that's Elliot, but it says Randolph Jeters."

"It's fake. Elliot lost his Com 2 license ten years ago due to substance abuse. His employment history has been sketchy since then. It has been hard to pin him down anywhere."

"It figures that Barber would be using a guy like him. He seemed a little shaky," Larry said.

"By the way, Barber and Elliot never left the plane. A helicopter took the Cessna to a CGM and our guys found them still in the plane. I guess you were lucky to get out," he said then he drank some coffee.

"You probably read that the water was really pouring in when I opened the door," Larry said.

"I'll bet it was. Did Brown tell you anything about this operation?"

"No, he didn't, but he's CIA, so I would expect that he wouldn't."

"This is strictly FYI. Anybody who knows will deny any knowledge of the events and call you a liar, in very polite terms, of course."

"That would certainly be a change. Can we get on with it."

"This was an attempt to steal the world's supply of Rhodium and 150 million dollars in cash. What were you told?"

"The recovery of two nuclear bombs and later I was told that that operation was a cover to stop an assassination attempt on the Secretary of State," Larry summarized.

"They used both stories to carry out their operations. The only sources of Rhodium are a small mine in Russia and a mine in Africa. Unfortunately, the mine in Africa is in a politically unstable country so the supply is currently stopped. Barber and some other people were running a big time con game. All the foreign money from the bomb recovery scam was used to finance their operation. The bombs were museum 'warbles'. They look real on the outside and are low density concrete on the inside, so it really didn't matter if the Arabs got a hold of them," Smith explained.

"There is the small matter of a few lives put in danger. Mine, the phony Joe Cole, the Portugese diver, mine, the six guys I killed in Thailand and Morocco, mine, Barber and Elliot. Did I mention mine?"

"We had to let the thing play out, of course. They were in foreign countries and you know the hassles of people seeking sanctuary outside the country and the news media wanting the story and names getting mentioned, yada, yada."

"Since I didn't get a return visit from Harrison, all's well I take it?"

The American money was hidden and we recovered it all. Thank goodness, because my ass was on the line here."

"It's a shame that I missed seeing you squirm," Larry quipped.

"Would you have liked to be the star in an open congressional hearing?"

"Like that Donald Rumsfeld Aspartame investigation? Do you know how fast that was shutdown?"

"Other than not bringing Barber back alive, you did a great job. We got a whole bunch of foreign nationals collared."

"Don't bother to thank me. I know that there wasn't 150 million dollars and ten railcars of Rhodium on that Cessna," Larry stated.

"There was a container with one and a half million dollars and a computer and computer discs that would allow them to run the operation from anywhere. Fortunately, the container was airtight. That saved us some time and trouble."

"Bully for you. I thought Barber was sounding awful disappointed, but when you're going down to ditch, people get emotional, I suppose."

"Yes, I'm sure that they do. You'll never guess what vessel was carrying the contraband Rhodium."

"I can imagine. All quiet on frontlines now? I can go home and chew milk duds and tell my friends all about my big adventure?" Larry asked.

"Like us, keep it under wraps for now. Your newspapers don't seem to like you too much anyway. One more thing, you will probably hear a story about Admiral Turnbull dying in a boating accident. Harvey tried to distance himself from his friend, Barber. He wanted an accident so his family can collect the insurance."

"Asshole Turnbull, servant of the people," Larry said.

"Even Hitler had family that loved him. I'll call you at home if I need to talk with you again," Smith said as they stood up.

"Stop by and say hello. People are so friendly on Nantucket," Larry said as they went through the door.

From Boston, he took the commuter to Memorial airport. Shirley picked him up there.

CHAPTER FIFTEEN

"Mom and rest of them send their love," Larry said as he took his luggage off of the four wheeler.

"How was the weather?"

"Pretty good. The last decent days of the years."

"I heard that Turnbull was killed in Annapolis. He was canoeing and a water skiing boat broadsided him. It didn't leave much, I guess," Shirley informed him.

"He paddled his canoe the wrong direction in this life," Larry remarked.

"Doubtless somebody's head will roll for it. You were lucky, this snow is getting a lot worse," Shirley said as they went through the exit doors and into the snow squall.

"But Doug Hamlicher has to be careful. He's sailing around the world, alone."

"Bully for him," Shirley said, always playing the straight man.

"Honey bear, his only comfort from the frozen sea is Nescafe," Larry insisted as he put his bags in the back.

"He wasn't alone. There was a camera crew there, filming him," she said as they got in the SUV.

"Busted! That is very perceptive of you. I guess that's why you were a Flight Lieutenant and I was just a Chief," Larry said, smiling.

Shirley started up the Gelaenderwagen and pulled out of the parking lot.

"I ran into darling Bruce. He implied that I married beneath me."

"That fucker just can't stop playing his head games," Larry said.

"He lost his job. You may not be seeing him for a while. Frank Folger and the rest of the gang thought that you were on another covert operation. I don't think they believed me when I told them that you just went back to Ohio this time."

"Funny you should mention that. Somebody went out of their way to tell me about Turnbull and a few other unfortunate fellows overseas. What, if anything, have we learned here?"

"To cut blocks and sew baby quilts. The only worthwhile thing a man ever taught me," Shirley quipped.

"You make me so fucking horny," Larry said.

When they came in the door, Rosa was holding Althea.

"Two suitcases were left on the porch. They looked like yours, so I opened them. Your clothes and your watch and shoes were in there," Rosa said.

Larry was happy that it hadn't exploded.

"Thanks. Have you been a bad girl," Larry said as he took the baby from Rosa then he softly bit her baby cheeks.

"She crawled over to the waste basket and tried to pull out her poopy diaper."

"Oh no! How's daddy gonna' get you married if you're doing things like that, huh?"

Later that evening, Larry was unpacking his suitcase when he found a computer disc. He knew it shouldn't have been in there. He put it in Shirley's laptop. He quickly realized it was a portion of the pre-fight commentary on the USS Ranger. One of the commentators was talking to the crowd on the hangar deck.

Commentator: What's your name?"

Sailor: Airmen First Class Derrick Long.

Commentator: "What did you think of meeting Ray Ronson?"

Long: "He was cool. He signed my Sleeve," Derrick said, showing the signature on his sleeve.

Commentator: "Are you betting on him?"

Long: "I wouldn't bet against the Master Chief. He is one of those 'old school' guys. You don't piss 'em off."

Commentator: Thank you. What's your name?"

Sailor: "Machinist Mate Haskill."

Commentator: I heard that Gooch Haynes, Ronson's manager, asked the Admiral for the toughest guy on the ship and the Admiral said it was Larry Mayer. What do you think of that?"

Haskill: "I'm surprised that the Chief would allow himself to do that."

Commentator: Do what?"

Haskill: "Come in contact with the lower classes."

Commentator: "Thank you. You look important. What's your name?"

Sailor: "Senior Chief Haroldson."

Commentator: And what do you think of this fight?"

Haroldson: "It's a mistake."

Commentator: "Why is that?"

Haroldson: "Larry is pure sailor. He doesn't engage in any contact sports unless it's with a woman."

Commentator: Thank you. The only place to settle this is in the ring. Back to you Chris."

'Old Hard Ass', you always told the truth even if was only your opinion, he thought. It's hard to be liked that way, but Larry had always treated him as a friend. Larry had told the truth, the 'no holds barred' truth, and now everybody is happy, if not friendly. The video disc was probably meant to show that somebody had done an extensive background check on him. He ejected the disc and put it back in the case. Brown or Smith must have been responsible for sending his luggage home, he thought. He heard Shirley greeting her father and stepmother at the front door. It was such a normal thing, at a normal house, on a normal day in a fucked up world.

"Hello, Albert," Larry said as they shook hands.

"Larry, staying out of trouble?" his father-in-law asked.

"With your daughter and your granddaughter here? You're joking, right?" Larry said.

"We just came from the indoor shuffleboard tournament. There's some real tough guys for ya'," he quipped.

"You know it. Once they've had their Metamucil they get vicious as can be," Larry added.

Later, at the dinner table-

"...so these two naked young women, they couldn't have been more than eighteen I'd guess, were running toward me, so I moved aside and let them by. Everybody is yelling 'Policia', I guess because I'm wearing Service Khakis..."

"Hold on, Larry! You're telling us that you went from being marooned on a desert island to being in the middle of a drunken orgy on a yacht in less than a half hour?" Joan asked incredulously.

"Yes, with a buffet and everything."

"I hope the food was good," Albert joked as he cut up his steak.

"Ghastly off-Island stuff. Is that cardiologist still giving you grief about red meat, dad?" Shirley asked.

"As always. What do you think, Larry?"

"Red meat is not bad for you. Blue-green meat, now that's bad for you," Larry said, smiling.

"That place in Hyannis doesn't win any medals for cooking," Joan complained.

"Oh, I forgot to tell you. Larry got another medal. A Silver Star for action in Bosnia in '92," Shirley said.

"Better late than never," Albert remarked.

"Not for Joe Cole, unfortunately."

In the gathering darkness, Larry and Joe watched the Serbian convoy of armored cars and trucks heading southwest.

"That's the column that wasted the village."

"Heading deeper into Bosnia. That's bold!" Larry remarked as he put on the face shield.

"Payback time," Joe said as he picked up his huge rifle.

"Get him the first time," Larry said as he got up cautiously with the flamethrower.

The truck rolled by just feet away from him when he heard the .50 caliber. He heard men shouting and he turned the napalm on them as they tried to get out of the back of the truck. A least one Serb cut loose on full auto with an AKM, but Larry had moved off to the side and emptied the tanks onto the truck as men, on fire, leaped out. Joe cut down the driver and the officer as they tried to flee. Larry jettisoned the empty tanks and made for the fallback position. Grateful to be relieved of eighty pounds, he scrambled over the boulders in the darkness with nothing but a .45 auto pistol belt and a flashlight which he dared not use.

By 0600, they were holed up in a cleft at the top of a cliff. They had constructed a blind of dirt and local vegetation and they thought it unlikely that they could be spotted from the air. A Russian made Mi-24 helicopter made a close pass then returned about ten minutes later. It stopped and hovered right above them.

"He's seen us, Chief," Joe said as he aimed Larry's M14 straight up at the helicopter.

"He can't see us from there. Those things are invulnerable to ground fire."

"I'll blow his balls off," Joe said then he shot two rounds at the underside of the helicopter.

The helicopter veered away rapidly. Joe handed the rifle to Larry and grabbed the .50 Barrett gun.

"Thanks for giving away our position," Larry said as he got into firing position.

The helicopter stopped about a hundred yards away and broadside to them. Larry saw the service panel below the jet engine. He knew that it covered oil coolers, so he aimed for them. He shot five rounds in as many seconds. Dark smoke began pouring out of the slits. Joe shot a .50 AP through the canopy. The helicopter suddenly turned toward them then rolled to the right and fell to the rocky slope below the cliff.

"Let's go collect our medals," Joe quipped as he gave Larry the field pack.

Larry hitched up the pack and grabbed his M14.

"Remember, it's not just a job, it's an adventure."

"Yeah, if we find that UN patrol. You can lose that big gun of yours," Larry said as he turned and headed south.

"Those Army bastards will have me paying for it."

"Scratch one flamethrower."

"No more favors for the Army. Let's go back to Diego."

"Thank that asshole Turnbull," Larry remarked.

"I told him that he's not interviewing me like I'm some fucking civilian."

"I told the XO to cram it," Larry quipped.

"I told him that I never dived with anybody I didn't trust. Same deal here."

"You hurt his one and only feeling."

"I took that page outta' your book. The old 'fuck them first' play."

"Too damn eloquent for a sailor in a combat zone," Larry opined.

"You've gotten mean since you got married," Joe said as he followed Larry between the rock walls.

"It's divorce that makes men mean," Larry quipped.

"Never married, hence never divorced. I couldn't be happier."

Later that day-

"....We made our way back on the indicated trail and met up with the Army patrol commanded by Specialist E5 Oliver Spracher at 1451 hours at the indicated location at the creek," Joe concluded, reading verbatim from their report.

"According to your report, you claim eighteen men killed at the ambush of the truck and at least the pilot of the helicopter killed," Lieutenant Commander Jackson stated.

"That is correct," Joe replied.

"You confirmed this, Master Chief?"

"Yes, I counted them myself," Larry replied.

"In the dark?"

"They were easy enough to see when they were burning."

Joe laughed at that.

"I see. You jettisoned the M2-2 before leaving the location. Is that correct?"

"Correct," Larry replied.

"You left a piece of equipment that could be used against American armed forces at a later date?" he asked accusingly.

"I threw it onto the flaming wreckage of the truck, so I highly doubt that it is of any use to the enemy."

"The Captain is unwilling to give you credit for the destruction of the Mi-24, since you did not actually see it crash," LtCdr Jackson stated.

"We feel that seeing it rolling while falling and the sound of it crashing and the smoke seen immediately afterward are sufficient evidence of its destruction," Joe stated.

"The Captain doesn't agree."

"I didn't see the Captain there in the mud and cold with us," Joe said rather tersely.

"I'll let him know that," Jackson said, adding-"So, we have the loss of one M2-2 incendiary projector, expenditure of two .50 caliber AP rounds and twelve rounds of 7.62 AP. Is that all there is to report?"

"Aye," they both replied.

"Since a team member is on report, the Captain is holding any submission for a citation per Navy regulations," Jackson informed them.

"Aye."

"That is all, gentlemen," Jackson said as they all stood up.

Larry and Joe saluted then they left the tent.

"I knew we'd get fucked over," Joe said.

"We'll redress grievances at a later date," Larry said.

"It was from somebody higher up. The president signed the citation," Shirley said.

His in-laws looked at Larry.

"I want the bucks. Give me the medal of honor."

"It's ten dollars a month, but you have to be sixty five to get it," Shirley said.

"We'll definitely have to get a picture," Joan said.

What a wonderful country, Larry thought to himself as he smiled at her.